A DEATH
IN THE
HAMPTONS

HATHERLEIGH PRESS
NEW YORK

A DEATH
IN THE
HAMPTONS

A NOVEL BY

MATT BLOOM

HATHERLEIGH PRESS
NEW YORK

Hatherleigh Press
5-22 46th Avenue, Suite 200
Long Island City, NY 11101
www.hatherleighpress.com

Printed in Canada

Library of Congress Cataloging-in-Publication Data To Follow

ISBN 1-57826-150-3

All Hatherleigh Press titles are available for bulk purchase, special promotions, and premiums. For more information, please contact the manager of our Special Sales department at 1-800-528-2550.

Jacket and interior designed by Dawn Velez-Le'Bron

FIRST PAPERBACK EDITION 2003

To New York City

Acknowledgements

I would like to thank my publishers, Andrew Flach and Kevin Moran; my editor, Margaret Miller, for her hard and patient work; Dawn Velez-Le´Bron, for a beautiful cover and interior design; my good friend, Scott Lax, for putting me up in his Chagrin Falls, OH home while I wrote the first draft; my parents, Joan and Robert; and my brother, Jonathan, for always having faith.

PROLOGUE

O ne day all of it will be gone: the houses, the people, even the land itself. Nothing has ever lasted here; not yet, anyway.

Before it became an island, it was part of the mainland, a coastal plain along the eastern seaboard of what would one day become the United States. For hundreds of millions of years, North America was located in the tropics, near the equator. Its eastern edge faced south, and off shore, a string of volcanic islands drifted closer until they finally collided with the continent. The massive collision pushed these volcanic rocks down deep, the intense pressure hardening them into the bedrock foundation of what is now called Long Island.

Africa drifted in next, eventually meeting North America head on, turning it to its present position. The two continents ground against each other and created the Appalachians, pushing them to heights beyond that of today's Rockies. Dinosaurs ruled then, and great rivers swept down from the new mountains, carrying huge deposits of sediment to the coast, piling it on top of the bedrock lying beneath the water. The weather also began to change, the heat giving way to an ice age. Some scientists say a meteor or asteroid hit the Earth, throwing up a huge dust cloud that blocked the sun, killed the dinosaurs and gave birth to massive glaciers in the arctic. The glaciers marched steadily south.

The land where Long Island stands today remained sub-merged until the glaciers captured much of the earth's water. The dinosaurs were then replaced by mammoths, mastodons and saber-tooth tigers. Fleeing the advancing glaciers, these creatures came to populate the coastal plain. And the glaciers kept coming, bulldozing much of Connecticut and dredging a giant river valley along the Atlantic.

The glaciers had covered the northern half of what would become Long Island by the time the climate began to warm again. The massive ice rivers began a slow retreat from the renewed heat, leaving behind hilly ridges on the north, two forks on the East End, and huge lakes like Ronkonkoma and Success where chunks of ice had gouged deep depressions. The temperature continued to rise and the ocean rose with it, eventually breaching the eastern and western edges of the river valley, turning it into a sound, and the high ground into an island.

Men first arrived on it many years later, having walked across the Bering Strait, then across the continent. They kept going until they reached Montauk Point and could go no further. The huge mammals that had succeeded the dinosaurs didn't last long against these skillful hunters, but much food remained in the form of fish and game and whales, as well as what the fertile soil produced. For centuries the Corchaug and Canarsie and Setauket and Montauket Indians thrived in this bountiful land, unaware that, just as for the dinosaurs and the mammoth before them, their days were numbered.

Their demise came at the hands of the Europeans, who arrived on boats bigger than any the Indians had ever seen. Giovanni da Verrazano was the first in 1524, followed by Henry Hudson almost a hundred years later, and Adrian Block soon after that. European influence and power spread steadily from the west end of the island to the east. The Indians had lost almost all of it by the late 1600's, their ranks decimated by disease and alcohol. The land they didn't lose in battle, they sold for trinkets and tools and promises.

Towns soon sprang up from New Amsterdam all the way to Montauk on the south fork, and Greenport and Orient on the north. These were mainly farming and fishing communities, dependent on the land and the sea for survival. The soil on the East End of the island stayed especially fertile and the surrounding waters remained stocked with fish. Whales were so abundant that, in the beginning, most were spotted and hunted right from the shore. They were later pursued in deep waters, from huge vessels that left Sag Harbor and returned several years later, if they returned at all. The whales became scarce by the end of the nineteenth century, and the whalers began to disappear. But the fishermen on this part of the island, bonackers, remained, each day gathering their livelihood from the bays and the ocean. For several hundred years, sons on the East End of Long Island followed their fathers out onto the water. Their sons, in turn, did the same.

But the beginning of the twentieth century brought change once again. New York artists and writers seeking to escape the city and gain inspiration discovered this part of Long Island and the towns there known as the Hamptons. Wealthy families soon followed them, and what had once been home to dinosaurs, then mammoths, then Indians, then farmers and fishermen, became a resort for the rich and the famous. But some of the farmers held onto their land and continue to work it. And a small number of fishermen remain to this day, pulling their living from the surrounding waters, too stubborn to leave, too rooted to their tradition to do anything else.

PART ONE

MEMORIAL DAY WEEKEND

CHAPTER

1

The overhead fans did little to disperse the heat. It had come early this year, settling like a damp blanket over Long Island's east end, making late May feel like mid-August. From his stool at Moran's, Andrew Kane watched the Sunday night movie on the TV over the bar. He had seen the movie before, but he watched it anyway, trying to keep his mind off what had happened that morning.

Things had been bad enough this year already. Fish prices were down and striped bass were scarce and new catch restrictions had put the squeeze on commercial fishermen all along the eastern seaboard. Andrew was used to it, though. As one of the few remaining baymen on Long Island, he'd spent most of his adult life struggling to put food on the table, chasing whatever happened to be running. If fish stocks were low, he'd scallop the Peconic, or clam the bays and inlets from Montauk all the way to the Shinnecock Canal. If the markets weren't paying enough for scallops and clams, he'd set lobster traps or float long lines for cod, tilefish and tuna. He used to go for swordfish, too, but nowadays most of them kept to deeper waters, and chasing them required more fuel than he was willing to buy. For this reason, Andrew had been staying in close, lately, rigging *Bessie* with a gill net and trolling her off Shagwong Point and Plum Gut. But he'd been catching mainly cheap fish there, blues and porgies and weakfish, nothing that put real money in his pocket.

The movie was an old Jack Hawker flick, and presently, Jack Hawker's rugged face filled the TV screen. He yelled "Die, scum!" while blasting machine gun rounds into unseen enemies. In no mood to watch the movie anymore, Andrew shifted his attention to Katie Moran, polishing a bottle of Old Grand Dad behind the bar. Katie had her back to him, and when her eyes met Andrew's in the mirror, he looked down into his glass of beer and studied the bubbles rising through it. He noticed that his hand, wrapped around the glass, was trembling ever so slightly.

Ralph Ludlow occupied the stool to Andrew's left. Ralph had given up commercial fishing ten years ago and converted his thirty-foot trawler into a charter boat. Now he took lawyers and doctors and accountants out on one-day trips. Ralph had never been a very good fisherman, commercial or otherwise. His customers usually didn't catch much and he rarely had repeat business.

"Think of it this way, Andrew," Ralph said. "The guy used to walk around talking and eating and farting, just like you and me. The only difference is, he went swimming and lost his head." Ralph grinned at his own joke.

"Thanks, Ralph. That's comforting."

Ralph shrugged and pulled the bill of his Yankees cap down lower.

"Just trying to help."

Donny Newton scratched on the eight ball and lost yet another game of pool. He returned to the bar and dragged on his cigarette, squinting the way he'd seen Bogart do it in *The Maltese Falcon*.

"He was murdered," he said to Andrew, taking the stool to his right. "No doubt."

"You think so?"

"Either that or a shark."

Andrew thought about it for a moment.

"But a shark wouldn't take just the head and leave the body."

"Not unless it was a thresher shark." Donny sliced his hand through the smoky air. "Tails like knives. One swipe's all it takes."

"More likely it was a propeller," Ralph said. "Some rich yahoo's yacht."

Andrew didn't want to talk about it anymore. He didn't want to think about it, either. The body he'd found that morning belonged to Seth Donahue, an actor he'd seen in a few movies. He'd netted it ten miles east of Montauk Point, just before dawn when the stripers were supposed to be running. But the stripers weren't, and, unlike fish, the body felt dead and heavy in his net. Winching it in, Andrew thought he might have caught a stray buoy or a piece of driftwood. He brought it in to *Bessie*'s stern, then turned on the flashlight and pointed it down to the water. And there he saw it, clothed in only a pair of green swim trunks, a gaping hole where its head should have been.

"It's a bad omen," Donny grumbled, stubbing out his cigarette. "I swear the South Fork is going to hell in a handbasket."

"Going?" Ralph said. "It's already there."

Katie came over and gave the bar in front of them a wipe-down.

"You guys catch anything today…besides dead bodies?"

She got no answer, only three dejected looks. She gave each of them a fresh bottle of Budweiser and emptied Donny's ashtray.

"You should quit smoking, Donny," she said.

"I know. These things are killing me."

"I don't care about that. I'm sick of emptying your ashtrays." Katie knocked her knuckles against the bar. "Those are on me."

Donny lifted his new beer.

"Here's to headless bodies, fellas."

"Could be a sign from God," Ralph offered.

"God can't afford it out here anymore," Andrew said.

"That makes two of us." Donny reached around Andrew and tapped Ralph's shoulder. "Let's shoot some pool. Dollar a game."

Andrew stayed on his stool while Donny and Ralph played. He finished his old beer, poured the new one, and looked up at the swordfish he'd caught years ago. He studied the fish's sleek lines and relived some of the battle. Then his eyes began to wander through Moran's. It hadn't changed much since his childhood, when his father let him run around it while he drank his pints. It had the same wooden floor as it did back then, and the same wooden bar, both worn by years of use. The walls were still covered with yellowed photos of fishermen beside the prizes they'd just caught. A decaying net drooped down from the ceiling, and a bleached shark jaw had been mounted over the entrance. It hung crooked now, ready to fall on some unsuspecting patron's head. Moran's had a few unsteady tables scattered around without any discernable order or plan, and its picture window faced northwest, providing its patrons with views of the sun setting over Fort Pond Bay and Gardiner's Island. Andrew watched it set almost every night.

The sky had just gone dark, but it seemed much later than eight-thirty. Andrew sneaked another look at Katie, who was reading the front section of the *New York Times* now, her dirty-blonde hair tied back in a ponytail. He couldn't recall the last time he'd seen it down and he wondered, as he often did, whether Katie would spend the rest of her life here.

He knew the history of the bar well—and how intertwined it was with Katie's own. Her great grandfather had built it before prohibition. Local lore contended that Old Man Moran served whiskey and beer to some of Roosevelt's Rough Riders, who had managed to sneak away from their quarantine near the railroad station. Moran's hadn't closed during Prohibition. It became a speakeasy instead, a gathering place for rum runners, gangsters, and the occasional fisherman with cash to spare after a good haul. Legend had it that the bar used to be rigged to pulleys so the liquor could be lowered and concealed beneath the floorboards in case of a raid. No patron had ever found the alleged hidden escape route, and Katie would never confirm nor deny its existence. Some said that the German spies who landed on the beach during WWII found their way to Moran's before being captured, but few believed that one.

Katie's grandfather took it over from Old Man Moran, then passed it on to Katie's father, who deeded it to Katie before he died a few years back. Andrew knew Katie could get a fair amount if she decided to sell the place. But she never accepted any offers, even though she threatened to at least once a week. Katie had no husband or children, and Andrew always figured that Moran's and its patrons helped to fill that void. Besides, he couldn't picture her living anywhere else but Montauk, or doing anything other than standing behind the bar, pouring drinks for her regulars.

"You need something, Andrew?" Katie said, still reading the paper.

"No, I'm fine."

"Could have fooled me."

Could have fooled me, too, Andrew thought, searching for something else to say to her, something funny, or at least clever. He'd known Katie since they were both six, growing up on Second House Road in Montauk. Thirty years later, he still felt shy around her, tongue-tied at times. He frequently remembered the first time he ever found her attractive, that day in eighth grade when he'd looked across the classroom and seen her differently than he ever had. And although she was no longer quite as pretty anymore, Andrew couldn't help looking at her whenever he had a chance to. Since his divorce a year ago, he found himself doing it more often.

He tried to forget about the body, but knew he wouldn't be able to very easily. He had radioed the police as soon as he caught it, and the ride back seemed much longer than it usually did. Pulling *Bessie* into Montauk Harbor, he saw Sheriff Pete Moran, Katie's uncle, waiting for him on the dock. Pete helped haul the body from the water and they stood looking down at it for a while, neither knowing what to say. Then Pete put his hand on the back of Andrew's neck.

"I'm glad your father wasn't here to see this," he said.

"Me too, Pete."

Pete slowly shook his head.

"Shit. I was hoping nothing like this would happen before I retired."

Andrew folded his arms on the bar and laid his head down on them. He closed his eyes, intending only to rest them. But he soon found himself in the middle of a raging storm, more powerful than any he'd ever been in. He struggled to guide *Bessie* through the fierce blow, wrestling her wheel as she crested each oncoming swell. The wind howled and the cold rain felt like sleet against his face. Lightning bolts ripped through the black sky, and beneath it, the sea began to boil and swirl, pulling *Bessie* into a whirlpool. Andrew held on as the vortex tightened and *Bessie's* spin gained speed, whipping the boat around and around and around.

Finally, the wind eased and the sky lightened and blued. *Bessie* slowed, then stopped spinning altogether. A hush settled over everything and the sea became calm and flat. Andrew released the wheel and removed his shirt. He used it to wipe the sweat and sea spray from his face. Then, out of the corner of his eye, he spotted a small object on the bow deck, quietly rocking with the boat's now-gentle motion.

He approached the object cautiously, and picked it up. It felt hard and solid and he began to untie the rags wrapped around it, peeling them off one by one. He sensed that something dangerous and frightening might lie beneath them, so when he got down to the last rag, he hesitated, then summoned the courage to pull it away. And there in his hands, he found his own head, his eyes bulging wide, his mouth frozen in a silent scream.

He woke suddenly and found his glass overturned, a puddle of beer spreading on the bar in front of him.

Katie looked up from her paper.

"You all right, Andrew?"

"Sorry, Katie. I'll clean it up."

Andrew mopped the spill with some bar napkins, his hands trembling even more now. He noticed how quiet and still Moran's had become. The TV had been shut off and it felt much hotter now. He turned to the pool table and found that Donny and Ralph and the rest of the patrons had gone. He heard someone say, "Bad dream, huh?"

He turned toward the voice and discovered a man with a long but rather wide face sitting two stools down from him. The man's black eyes matched the color of his hair, combed back with the aid of some kind of gel or mousse. He had a deeply cleft chin and, even in the barroom dim, he looked somewhat familiar.

"What were you dreaming about?" the man said. "Your mother-in-law?"

Andrew rubbed his eyes and looked at him more closely.

"Say, you're not—"

"Jack Hawker? Yeah, I am. Don't fall off your stool or anything."

"This is unbelievable," Andrew said, unsure if he was still dreaming or not. "I was just watching one of your movies on TV."

Jack glanced up at the set over the bar.

"I think it's Jack Hawker Week on Channel Nine," he said. "What's your name?"

"Andrew Kane."

"Sounds kind of biblical. Have a beer, Andrew Kane."

He slide a fresh bottle of Budweiser to Andrew and drank from his glass of Irish whiskey. Andrew took a sip of the beer, still wondering if his dream had merely shifted location and storyline.

"I take it you're a fisherman," Jack said.

"Good guess."

"It wasn't too hard."

What's he doing in here? Andrew thought.

"So, any new movies coming up?" he said.

Jack had to think about it.

"*Infinite Mayhem* will be out in the fall. The highest body count of any movie ever made."

"Sounds bloody."

"Nothing gratuitous, though. How's the fishing been?"

Andrew almost told him about finding Seth Donahue's body, but decided not to.

"There aren't as many fish as there used to be," he said.

"That's too bad."

"I'd rather have your job, to be honest."

Jack smiled into his whiskey.

"It has its drawbacks, believe it or not."

"That's hard to believe."

"Put it this way, its nice being around a real person like you, for a change. You shoot pool, Andrew?"

"I'm not bad."

"Let's play, then."

They went over to the pool table, its felt torn and stained by years of bad shots and spilled drinks. Jack inserted two quarters into the slot and pushed it in. The balls tumbled into the tray and Andrew racked them. Jack shot hard as soon as Andrew lifted the triangle, dropping two solids off the break. He proceeded to run the table, banking the eight into the side pocket to win.

"You're good," Andrew said, leaning on his unused cue.

"I get lucky every now and then."

Andrew racked again and Jack broke, sinking another solid. He sank his first three balls after that, and missed his fourth. Andrew shot and missed and Jack lined up the two ball, but seemed to lose interest before taking the shot. He straightened up and looked at Andrew.

"You seem troubled," he said. "If you don't mind me saying."

"I think I'm a little nervous being around a movie star. That's all."

Jack line up his shot again.

"Picture me in my underwear. That usually works." He sank the two ball. "Tell me about yourself, Andrew."

Andrew shrugged.

"There's not much to tell."

"I doubt that."

"I fish in the morning and drink beer at night. What else can I say?"

"Sounds like you need a little variety." Jack nudged the cue ball and it bumped the five into the corner pocket. "You know, I took this acting class years ago when I was first starting out. Each day the teacher would pair us with a different person and you had to tell him his life story just by reading his face and body language."

"Seems difficult," Andrew said, wondering why Jack had told him that.

"I got good at it after a while."

"How would you read me, then?"

Jack looked Andrew over.

"You're a man who's had a few disappointments," he said. "That's clear."

"Me and everyone else."

"I'll get more specific, if you want."

"Go ahead."

Jack looked at Andrew again, longer this time.

"Okay. You said the fish aren't running, right? No fish means no money. I don't see a ring on your finger, so either you never married or you're not married anymore. I'm guessing it's the latter, which means you're probably paying alimony. I'll go out on a limb and say you pay child support, too. That's not to mention fishing licenses, fishing taxes, permits, fuel, a mortgage on your boat, and credit card debt building up. On the emotional side, I bet there's a whole other life you wish you could have, maybe one that kind of slipped away from you. Sort of a close but no cigar kind of thing."

A chill ran up Andrew's spine. Jack had gotten him right, mostly. He wondered if someone, perhaps Donny, was playing a prank on him.

"Not bad," he said.

"You're an easy one, Andrew. No offense."

Jack leaned over the table again and sank the rest of his balls, one by one. He dropped the eight into the corner pocket with a hard, straight shot.

"Normally the loser buys," he said. "But I'll get the next round if you care to join me."

"Sure, why not?"

They went to the bar and Katie brought their drinks.

"And how are you tonight, sweetheart?" Jack said to her.

"I've been worse," Katie answered, ignoring Jack's extended hand. She returned to her newspaper.

"Tough cookie," Jack said to Andrew.

"Only on the outside."

Andrew glanced down at Katie. She looked particularly good tonight. He kept his eyes on her longer than he usually dared to.

"What are you thinking about?" Jack said, noticing the aim of Andrew's attention. "The one that got away?"

"There's always one getting away if you're a fisherman."

"I suppose you're right. It's a sad way to live, if you ask me."

Andrew turned to Jack and noticed the beginning of a smirk on his face.

"Sad? How do you figure?"

"Unfulfilling would probably be a better word."

Andrew turned away and drank in silence for a minute. He couldn't contain his irritation any longer than that. He turned to Jack again.

"Who are you to judge my life?" he said.

Jack pretended to be shocked.

"Don't flatter yourself, Andrew. I didn't even know you existed until half an hour ago."

"I'm not flattering myself. I just don't like to be insulted."

Jack's shock transformed into a condescending grin.

"Inarticulate working-class rage," he said. "That's good. Kind of like Stanley Kowalski in *Streetcar*."

Andrew tried to remember who Stanley Kowalski in *Streetcar* was.

"Well, you and Stanley Kowalski can both go fuck yourselves," he said, still unsure.

"I would if I could." Jack glanced down at his crotch. "From what the ladies tell me, I'm pretty damned good."

Andrew didn't know how to respond to that. He couldn't help smiling.

"See, Andy, you're not really mad at me," Jack said. "There's just a little displacement going on here. A little frustration."

Andrew felt the rest of his anger dissipate.

"Sorry about that," he said.

"It's okay. I admit I can be a bit honest sometimes. And I haven't been completely forthcoming with you."

"What do you mean?"

"What I mean is I'm not just having a drink here at good old Moran's." Jack drank some of his whiskey, as if to illustrate. "My next movie's going to be shot here on the South Fork this summer. It's called *A Death in the Hamptons*. I'll be playing a local fisherman and I need to do some research, learn the nuances."

"Nuances?"

"Mannerisms."

"Oh, mannerisms. What's the movie about?"

"Some fisherman who becomes an alcoholic after his wife leaves him. No, she leaves him because he becomes an alcoholic. The usual shit. I think his dog dies, too."

"And you want me to be your guinea pig."

"You're the real McCoy, Andrew, not a guinea pig. How many people can say that about themselves?"

Andrew gestured to the empty bar.

"Anyone in this bar can."

"Well, I can't. I'm just a phony baloney actor. I envy you. I really do."

"Spare me the crap, Jack. You wouldn't trade places with me for all the money in the world."

"That I already have, my friend. And then some." Jack studied his whiskey for a moment before looking up again. "I propose we hang out, Andrew, just like friends. What do you think?"

"Is that how friendship works with you show biz types?"

"Hey, we do the best we can. It's not always easy. What do you say? You might even have fun, for a change."

Fun. Andrew tried to remember the last time he'd had any.

"For how long?" he said.

"For as long as you like."

Andrew tried to think of reasons why he shouldn't, beside the fact that he didn't particularly like Jack Hawker very much. But how often does an opportunity like this come along? he thought, looking down the bar at Katie once again, imagining living the rest of his life without ever even trying to win her heart. He pictured himself dying here on his stool, or even ending up like Seth Donahue. He turned to Jack and noticed the bloodshot surrounding the black cores of his eyes. Before he could speak, Jack winked at him and said, "What do you say, Andy boy? We'll have some fun."

CHAPTER 2

Karla Sands leaned on her horn. That didn't cure her frustration. Nor did it move any of the cars jammed bumper to bumper on the Long Island Expressway. She reached over and petted Furball, asleep in the passenger seat.

"I'm not going to lose my temper this time, Furball," she said, running her fingers over the Yorkshire Terrier's meticulously brushed coat. "Mommy Goddess promises not to lose it."

She straightened the pink bow tied atop Furball's head, then looked at the minivan in the next lane. It contained a father, a mother, and their two young children. They reminded Karla of the family in a Disneyworld commercial she'd once seen.

"Who are these people, Furball?" she said, feeling somewhat contemptuous of them and their anomynity. "What godforsaken suburb did they come from?"

She honked again and the driver got out of the car in front of her. He walked toward Karla's BMW and Karla took in a deep breath, anticipating his body odor. She lowered her window and the hot, asphalt-scented breeze rushed in, ruining her air-conditioned cocoon. Furball let out a string of high-pitched yelps.

"Shhh, Furball! I can handle this myself."

Furball quieted and Karla smiled fakely at the dumpy, per-spiring man now standing beside her car. "Can I help you?"

"You gotta problem with your horn?"

Karla honked it.

"It sounds like it's working fine," she said.

"I can hear that. Do me a favor. Don't use it anymore. It ain't doing any good."

It is if it discourages clods like you from driving out to the Hamptons, Karla thought.

"Sorry. I'm in a bit of a rush," she said.

"Aren't we all, lady?"

The man returned to his car and Karla raised her win-dow. The traffic moved a few car lengths and stopped again. Karla almost hit the horn but instead pinched her thumbs and index fingers into circles and took three long, slow yoga breaths. Feeling somewhat calmer, she checked her watch. 8:30 pm. Dean and Simone Tropper's Memorial Day party started at nine. Dean had amassed a fortune in the family real estate business, so no expense would be spared. And Tropper parties always attracted an interesting crowd. Karla poked Furball's ribs and Furball looked at her with her big beady eyes and her tiny ham-colored tongue dan-gling from her mouth.

"This is a big weekend for me, Furball," Karla said. "I have to keep my eyes peeled because if I don't write good columns this summer, I'm through, kaput, yesterday's news. Understand?"

Furball cocked her head, in doggy sympathy.

"Your Mommy Goddess is a very talented lady, you know," Karla continued. "Not just anybody can do what your Mommy Goddess does. Not just anybody can write about the rich and famous like I do. Most people would kill to have my job, absolutely kill. I bet even you want my job. Well, you can't have it, Miss Furball. Don't even think about it."

Karla patted the dog's head and smiled, thinking about how well she managed to walk the tightrope—using the subjects of her columns while maintaining their trust, exposing just the right balance of their virtues and vices. Not an easy task, she thought with satisfaction. It's an art more than a craft, really. She checked her makeup in the rear view and wondered if her face had gained weight since yesterday.

The traffic started to move again, and in a few miles the terrain flattened, the pines on either side shrinking as the soil became more sand than dirt. Karla passed through the forest that had burned several years ago, rows and rows of charred, leafless trunks. Low underbrush had sprung up, but it would take years for the forest to fully restore itself. Like most everyone else, Karla used to get off the expressway at exit 70, the ramp circling past the big orange sculpture that looked like nothing in particular. But *Suzy's Hamptons Shortcuts* guidebook taught her that taking exit 71 to Route 24 is much faster. Fewer people took Route 24, which wound through Riverhead and Flanders, past the giant duck advertising the poultry farm that had been there for years. Karla had read that lightning once struck the duck, blowing its glass eyes right out of its concrete head. She pictured that image every time she drove past it.

Route 24 led her to the Montauk Highway, where the traffic moved as slowly as it had on the LIE. The highway crossed the Shinnecock Canal and a few miles and a half hour later, it narrowed to two lanes feeding into the Hamptons. There has to be a better way to get here, Karla thought, crawling past Southampton, knowing she still had to inch through Water Mill, Bridgehampton, Wainscott, and East Hampton, as well. Beyond East Hampton, Amagansett, Napeague and Montauk completed the string of South Fork towns. They looked similar to each other, seemingly as all-American as Norman Rockwell paintings, with a hint of salt in the air. But closer inspection would reveal nothing particularly quaint or rustic about them. Those seeking a country retreat might feel a bit cheated and deceived upon finding Gucci, Betsy Johnson and Ralph Lauren stores lining both sides of the road. The Hamptons offered no escape from New Yorkers, either. They flocked there by the thousands each summer weekend, their type-A demeanors only sharpened by a two-day time constraint and the arduous journey to and from.

Karla turned on the radio and scanned the stations until her tuner picked up some local news on WEHM. The top story was about Seth Donahue, one of the actors in the movie to be filmed in Montauk and the Hamptons this summer. His headless body had been found in the water early that morning.

"That sucks, doesn't it, Furball," Karla said. "They'll have to get someone else for his part. Who do you think would be good? What about Brad Pitt?"

She turned off the radio and found a Sugar B CD amongst the ones scattered on the dashboard. She put it on and selected the song called "Summer Of Dirt." And as she listened to Sugar B singing the refrain: "... Girl, don't be giving me no sass, 'cause I'll bust a cap right up yo' ass," an idea came to her.

"This will be my summer of dirt, too," she said. "What do you think of that, Furball? Everyone and everything's going to be fair game. No more Mr. Nice Girl. And you know what I'm going to tell them at *Boulevard* when I negotiate my contract in September? Are you interested at all, Furry? Well, I'm going to tell them that people buy *Boulevard Magazine* because of me, Karla Sands. They don't give a rat's ass about some Wall Street tycoon's apartment. They read my column to find out about his insider trading. They don't care about some actress's support for some ridiculous charity. They'd rather know who she's fucking to get her roles. It's my column they pay for, not the fluff pieces." She looked at her dog. "Mommy Goddess is going to demand more money in

September. A lot more money. What do you think of that, Furball?"

The traffic gained speed past the Water Mill light, but congealed again in Bridgehampton where the sidewalks were already crowded with people dressed in their casual weekend best. Karla's eyes shifted rapidly from one side of the street to the other, instinctively searching for information. She noticed the actor, Ted Courcik, walking with his model girlfriend, who went by the name Pia. Ted's as queer as a three dollar bill, Karla thought, with a smirk. His relationship with Pia is nothing more than a shameless publicity stunt.

She spotted Ivan Wilton a block further on. He had a tall, blonde woman on his arm. Karla lowered her window.

"Ivan! Where the fuck were you the other night?"

Ivan turned. He didn't seem happy to see Karla.

"Which night?"

"Ethan's book party at BookHampton!"

"I was in St. Bart's. At the house."

"St. Bart's, St. Farts. You missed a damned good party! Are you going to the Tropper's tonight?"

Ivan shrugged and the blonde grasped his arm more tightly and pulled him toward Billy Starr's entrance.

"Maybe I'll see you there," Ivan said, before disappearing into the restaurant. Karla pulled a mini-recorder from her Prada bag. She pressed the "Record" button with her tongue:

"9:15 pm. Friday, May 23rd. Trust fund prick, Ivan Wilton, going into Billy Starr's with some bimbo. I'm sure she's paying him for the meal in some creative way. Or maybe *he's* paying *her*. Look into it."

Karla reached East Hampton at quarter to ten. She turned off the highway just past the windmill, went through the underpass and made a sharp right into the Sasha and Joe's parking lot. It had already filled with an assortment of BMW's, Mercedes, Lexus and Jaguars, as well as two "look at me" cars, meticulously restored relics driven for the sole purpose of drawing attention, envy and admiration to their owners. Of course, cars aren't the only "look at me" commodity in the Hamptons. Houses, women, dogs, children, and even maids are also on display like so much flashy jewelry, particularly during the summer months.

Karla parked in the "No Parking" zone in front of Sasha and Joe's, a one-story brick structure, very modest considering its stature as one of the hottest restaurants in the Hamptons. She found Marcus, dressed in a tuxedo, at his podium just inside the door.

"Karla!"

"Marcus."

Marcus came from behind the podium and they exchanged a double-cheek kiss. Marcus stepped back and beamed at her.

"I was just thinking to myself, 'Now where's my dear friend, Karla Sands? She must being coming to see me this weekend.'"

"I was thinking the same thing, sweetheart. How was your winter, Marcus?"

"Very good." Marcus patted his stomach. "But I think I stored a few too many nuts."

Karla glanced at his belly bulging against his waistband.

"Don't be silly. You look great. Any news on the acting front?"

"Lots of auditions, but no parts yet."

"I'm sure that will change. I have such confidence in you, Marcus. Supreme confidence."

Not only fat, but balding too, Marcus didn't fit the image of an aspiring actor, nor that of maitre d' of a hip joint like Sasha and Joe's. He'd been there for years, though, due mainly to his copious glad handing and shameless ass-kissing. Marcus knew just how to make the rich feel richer and the famous feel more famous. He knew how to make the semi-important feel like masters of the universe. Over the years, he'd flattered, complimented and back-slapped a long list of Hampton elites into considering him to be a friend and a trusted confidant. His plan to parlay these friendships into an acting career had gotten him an agent, but not much else.

"Do you have a minute, Marcus?"

"For you, Karla, I have an hour."

Marcus snapped his finger at a waiter and ordered him to cover his post at the podium. He took Karla by the elbow and guided her to the bar.

"Joseph, get Miss Sands a drink," he barked at the man behind it.

"Pellegrino," Karla said to Joseph. "With a twist of lemon."

"Maybe I would be thinner if I only drank water like you," Marcus said.

"Don't be ridiculous. You wouldn't be you if you didn't carry a little heft. It's sexy, if you ask me."

This brought a twinkle to Marcus's eyes. Karla worried she might have gone too far with that lie.

"We had a good thing going last summer," she said, altering her tone to strictly business.

"Very good, if I remember correctly," Marcus said, matching her tone.

Joseph brought the water and Karla waited for him to leave.

"I want to continue our arrangement, if that's agreeable to you," she said. "Two hundred dollars per item. That's what I was paying you, wasn't it?"

"Karla, discussing money with a good friend always makes me a little uncomfortable."

"Pretend I'm your worst enemy, then."

"How about two-fifty, then? My daughter needs braces this year."

"Braces for what?"

"Her teeth. They're crooked."

Karla rolled her eyes.

"That's tough. Two hundred. No more. And I want good shit. Solid. No gossip or hearsay. I'll give you two minutes to decide."

Marcus's eyes dropped to his sleeve. He picked some lint off it.

"Okay," he said. "Two hundred."

"Two hundred it is. You have my numbers, right?"

Marcus forced a smile.

"I never forget a name, a face, or a number."

"That's why I'm here . . . besides the fact that I love you dearly."

"Karla, you're making me blush."

"Don't do that. It doesn't go with your tux. What's your daughter's name?"

Marcus smiled again, naturally this time.

"Patricia," he said.

"Well, you get me enough dirt this summer and Patricia's teeth will be straight in no time."

"You know, you should have a child some day, Karla. You'd make a wonderful mother."

Karla drank some water and crunched an ice cube between her molars.

"You think so?"

"Absolutely."

"Maybe next year. Listen, I have to get going. The Troppers are having a party."

Marcus's eyes lit up again.

"The Troppers! Tell them to come see me soon. I always give them the best table."

"How much does that cost them?"

"Karla, please."

"Sorry. I couldn't resist." Karla indicated the door with her chin. "You better take care of your customers, Marcus."

They double cheek-kissed again and Karla left Marcus at the bar. Give it up, fat boy, she thought on her way out. There won't be a part for you in any movie, not unless they make one about a greedy, two-faced, back-stabbing suckup of a maitre d'. If they ever do, you'll probably win the Oscar. She took a mint from the bowl by the door, then considered the calories and dropped it to the floor. She left the restaurant and got back in her BMW.

"Did you miss Mommy Goddess, Furball?"

Furball didn't bother to raise her head off her paws.

"You didn't miss me?" Karla said. "Well, fuck you, too."

She flicked her finger against the end of Furball's nose, then put on "Summer of Dirt" again and cranked it loud. She hit the gas and burned some rubber pulling out of the parking lot.

CHAPTER

3

Jack parked his Porsche in front of Dean Tropper's house on West End Road. Tropper owned the largest place on Georgica Pond, white and modern, mostly glass panes and clean lines. It had been designed by Hoshi Subuki, Japan's most celebrated architect, and it was featured in the May issue of *Vacation Estate Magazine*. Jack found a tan blazer in the back seat and handed it to Andrew.

"Put this on, Andrew. And tuck in."

They got out and Andrew put the blazer on over his flannel shirt and ripped jeans. He and Jack were almost exactly the same size, so it fit perfectly. He tucked in.

"Just be yourself," Jack said, as they walked toward the house. "And don't let anyone intimidate you."

They went inside and found Dean Tropper greeting his guests with a highball in one hand and a slab of filet mignon in the other. Dean had a round face and a semi-circle of dark hair around his otherwise bald head. He wore no shoes and stood only five foot four in stocking feet.

"Glad you could make it, Jack," he said, a bite of filet bulging his left cheek.

"I wouldn't miss it," Jack said. "How's the steak?"

"I stole it from the kitchen before they could cut it into little girly slices." Tropper held the meat out to Jack. "Want some?"

"No, thanks."

Tropper gave the filet in his mouth a few more chews.

"Have you seen my new Tropper Tower West yet, Jack? Third tallest residential in the world. Like a big schvantz on the Hudson River. You want to take a floor?"

"I'll think about it."

"Tell me yes now and I'll give you a quarter off market price." Tropper stood on his toes and peered over Jack's shoulder, at Andrew behind him. "Who's your friend?"

Jack stepped aside.

"Dean Tropper, meet Andrew Kane. Andrew's my fisherman buddy."

"No shit. I fish, too," Tropper said. "Caught a big marlin down in St. John this winter. Fucking thing didn't stand a chance, not against The Deano."

"Marlins are tough fish," Andrew said.

"Speaking of tough fish, you guys hear they found Seth Donahue in the water this morning?"

"I heard about it," Jack said. "Too bad."

Andrew's hands began shake again, and he felt a little weak-kneed now. He was picturing Donahue's mutilated body, smelling its rancid odor. Tropper took another bite of meat and spoke with his mouth full.

"They're not sure what happened to him yet," he said. "I think they used a birthmark on his ass to ID him. Kind of throws a monkey wrench into the movie you're making here, doesn't it, Jack?"

"That it does," Jack said. "Seth was perfect for the part."

Andrew managed to swallow back a wave of nausea.

"You all right there, Andrew?" Tropper said. "You look ready to puke."

"I'm okay, thanks."

"Have a drink. Booze always settles my stomach." Tropper

indicated the bar across the room. "You guys help yourselves. Just leave some for me. Ha! Ha!"

Like the exterior of his house, Tropper's cavernous living room looked sparse and minimalistic, not a place most people would feel comfortable spending much time in. It had a high ceiling and a marble floor divided into alternating black and white squares. The furniture looked too new to sit on; most of the guests were standing. Water sheeted down one wall into a pool filled with tropical fish. A large canvas painted entirely blue covered another wall, and a stainless steel sculpture of a bull stood near the back. A glass dome in the ceiling allowed a view of the night sky, and just like at Moran's, a picture window looked out at the ocean, which reflected a moon path all the way to the horizon.

The room had already filled with Dean's guests, clustered into knots of conversation. But few of them seemed completely focused on who they were speaking to, their eyes flitting around, looking for someone better or more interesting. Andrew had never seen so many good-looking women in one place, never so many wearing designer dresses and expensive-looking jewelry. He followed Jack toward the bar, self-conscious about his clothes despite the blazer Jack had lent him. Halfway there, a large-breasted woman stepped in front of them, blocking their way.

"I heard what you did at Petruska, you devil," she said, shaking her finger at Jack.

"That was nothing," Jack said. He slapped the woman's ass as he moved past her. At the bar, he ordered a Jamesons and a Budweiser, which he gave to Andrew.

"I told you not to be intimidated," he said.

"I'm not."

"Then why are your hands shaking?"

Loud laughter drew their attention to the actor, Allen Balford, who stood in the middle of a small group that had gathered around him.

"No, seriously," Balford said, running his hand through his shoulder-length, dirty-blond hair. "I shouldn't joke about it.

I mean, I really feel badly for Seth. What a way to go. I feel badly for Francis, too. He has to fill that role fast."

"How about you, Allen?" a small, severe-looking woman said. "I think you'd be perfect for the part."

"C'mon, Karla, I couldn't. That would be in bad taste."

"Someone has to do it."

Balford thought about it for several moments, then lifted his martini glass.

"That's true," he said, before drinking. "Why not me?"

Gwendolyn Pavlik emerged from the crowd. Andrew recognized her angular face, her sunken cheeks beneath her high cheekbones. She had played the femme fatale in two of Jack's movies. She kissed Jack on the lips and hooked her arm through his.

"I need it, Jack," she whispered, loudly.

"Now?"

"Now."

Jack turned to Andrew.

"I'll be back. Don't get into any trouble."

He left with Gwendolyn and Andrew found a spot against the wall beneath a large mountain-scape painting with the word "Yeah" written in different fonts all over it. He stood there drinking his beer and surveying the party, feeling like a man who had somehow wandered into the film he'd been watching. The fact that he recognized some of the guests from movies he'd seen, only strengthened this perception.

Two slightly drunk young men in blue blazers stepped up to the bar. They ordered gin and tonics, and with the drinks, they moved to a spot next to Andrew.

"I'm telling my clients that Incore stock is going to be in the toilet soon," the taller one said to his companion, speaking quietly. "Technology is the way to go."

"Tell me something I don't know."

"All right. Get this. A friend of mine is friends with a guy who knows a scientist working for AmerGentech, a small biotech."

"Never heard of it," the shorter one said.

"You will. Trust me. So, this scientist passes a little information to his friend who passes it to my friend who passes it to me." The taller man lowered his voice. "Word is AmerGentech's on the verge of perfecting a drug that allows humans to live longer—thirty to forty years longer."

The shorter one raised his right eyebrow.

"You're kidding."

"I kid you not. It improves cell regeneration or something."

"Sounds crazy."

"Sounds good to me. You interested?"

The shorter man pondered the proposition.

"I might be," he said.

"If you are, call me at the office Monday morning. Say, you hear about Seth Donahue, that actor?"

"Yeah. I don't think this new AmerGentech drug could have helped him much, not unless it regrows heads, too."

The two men shared a laugh.

Until coming to this party, the stark reality of finding Seth Donahue's body had begun to soften for Andrew, like a dream fading from memory. Now, he couldn't escape it. The picture window promised some distraction, so he made his way over to it and looked out at a large, well-maintained lawn. It rolled and sloped like a golf course, stretching all the way to the beach. Ground lights and the moon, blurred and reddened by thick humidity, illuminated the grassy expanse. The fishing should be good tonight, Andrew thought, looking at the ocean beyond the lawn, not sure if he'd ever want to go out on it again.

He left the window and headed back to the bar. He considered trying the champagne, but ordered another Budweiser. He wandered again, unsure where to go or who to talk to, still self-conscious about his clothes. He noticed that the crowd filling the room was actually a gathering of small, distinct groups, temporary alliances that broke apart and reformed into new ones every few minutes. He heard someone say, "David Bouley couldn't cook his way out of a paper bag." He heard someone else say, "You have to join me in Bermuda, Roger. We'll sail down there on my yacht." He passed a fat man waving an American Express Black Card under a thin man's nose. "This is as close as you'll ever get to one of these," the fat man said. A tall woman who looked like a model slapped the face of a woman who might have been her twin. Andrew kept moving and noticed the only non-whites at the party, three black men standing beside each other, their arms folded across their chests. Each wore dark, wraparound sunglasses, a shiny purple suit and an impassive expression. A smiley white woman bounded up to the smallest one, flanked by the other two.

"Sugar B!" she said, giving him a hug.

Sugar B kept his arms folded and he maintained his non-expression.

"Yassup?" he said.

"I just wanted to tell you, your new album is so dope. It's really helping me understand the ghetto experience."

Sugar B nodded.

"That's cool."

"No, really. It must be so hard being African-American in America."

"Oh, it ain't so bad." Sugar B slipped his arm around the woman's waist. "'Least not for me."

Andrew found a table of hors dourves, each with a detailed label in front of it. He ate two filet mignons on toasted French toast and a smoked salmon slice with chopped dill. He avoided the miniature white truffle quiches and the tuna carpaccio garnished with edible flowers. He considered trying some of the sushi, the pieces arranged in a crude replica of Dean Tropper's smiling face. He took a shrimp instead and dunked it in some wild plum and anchovy sauce. As he lifted it to his mouth, he was suddenly assaulted with an embrace from a woman wearing a short blue dress.

"Mark!" she said, beaming pure joy at him.

"No, I'm Andrew."

"Are you sure?"

"Last time I checked."

The woman began to laugh.

"If you change your mind, Mark, come talk to me." She eyed Andrew's clothes. "By the way, I like the look. Very shabby ultra hip chic." She turned from Andrew and joined an artistic-looking group. "Julian, Julian, Julian! I am sooo drunk! Promise not to let me make a complete fool of myself tonight."

Andrew felt someone tap his shoulder. He turned and found the woman Allen Balford had called Karla standing next to him.

"And you are?" Karla said, in a clipped, business-like tone.

"Excuse me?"

Karla stepped closer to Andrew and looked up into his face, as if trying to memorized his features.

"Your name. What is it?"

"Andrew Kane."

"You're a friend of Jack Hawker's?"

"I don't know if you'd call us friends."

"Well, I saw you come in together. How long have you known him?"

"Only a couple of hours."

"That's long enough. What do you do?"

"I'm a fisherman."

A smile tugged at Karla's thin lips, but it didn't get any further than that.

"That's very noble of you," she said. "Do you know who I am?"

"I don't think so."

"I'm Karla Sands, a columnist for *Boulevard Magazine*. Ever read it?"

"No."

"You should. You might learn something." Karla pulled a business card from her handbag and handed it to Andrew. "Call me if you see anything I might be interested in. I'll make it worth your while."

Karla walked off just as Jack reappeared with lipstick marks on both cheeks.

"What did that bitch want?" he said.

"I'm not sure."

"The less you say to these vultures, the better. That's my advice to you."

Allen Balford broke away from a well-kept elderly woman who had managed to corner him. He quick-stepped over to Jack and stood next to him, as if for protection.

"I swear that old coot Swensen is trying to get her hands down my Jockeys," he said, a disgusted look on his face.

"Why don't you let her?"

"I don't need the money *that* badly. My career's not dead yet."

"It's not?"

Balford gave Jack a sideways look.

"You might be climbing down the old ladder one day yourself, Hawker."

"I wouldn't bet on it."

"Is Jack Hawker a cocky bastard? The survey says yes."

Jack turned to Balford.

"What do you want, Allen?"

"As long as we're not beating around the bush, I'm aware you're gonna have to find someone to fill Seth's part."

"Shame, isn't it?"

"Damn shame. Listen, Jack, what do fishermen do? They stand around looking at the water. I can play one in my sleep."

"Lots of guys can."

"But I still have a name. And I can act."

Jack let out a short laugh.

"That's debatable," he said. "What do you want me to do? I'm not the director."

"But you're the star and the executive producer."

"It's Francis's decision."

"Then talk to him. Put in a good word for me."

"What's in it for me, Allen?"

Balford flashed a big, phony smile and spread his arms, as if preparing to hug Jack.

"You get to work with Allen Balford, baby," he said. "That's what's in it for you."

Jack stifled a yawn.

"All right. I'll talk to Francis. Just remember I did you a favor."

"Jack, this is Allen Balford you're dealing with. Allen Balford never forgets a good deed. Ask anybody. And by the way, you were fucking awesome in *Blood Precinct.*"

Allen made a playful pistol shooting gesture at Jack, then headed off. But he spun around after taking a few steps.

"We'll be catching all kinds of fish this summer," he said, miming a cast and reel. "Know what I mean, Jack?"

Balford spotted a group of young women, all of them drinking cosmopolitans from large martini glasses. He sauntered over to them.

"Okay, which one of you beauties is going to sleep with Allen Balford tonight?" he said, loudly.

Jack put his hand on Andrew's shoulder.

"You look bored, my man."

"Not at all."

"Well, I am. Come with me. I'll show you around."

A wide, spiral staircase corkscrewed to the second floor. Jack and Andrew made their way up it, and the staircase left them at the beginning of a long hallway with closed doors on either side.

"So, Mr. Tropper made his money in real estate?" Andrew said, trying to make conversation.

"Tropper's father made Tropper's money," Jack answered. "Dean just screws people out of more of it."

The hallway seemed endless and the chatter and laughter from the party below faded as they proceeded down it. Jack fell a step behind Andrew, and when they got to the end of the hallway, he directed Andrew into another, equally as long. How many rooms could two people possibly need, Andrew wondered as he passed each door. When he reached the end of the second hallway, he turned to Jack.

"A lot of rooms in this—"

But Jack had disappeared. Andrew spun around and found the hall empty behind him.

"Jack! Hey, Jack!"

No answer or sign of him. Then the door of the last room on the right opened a crack and a woman in a tight Chinese-style dress peeked out of it. She had long, dark hair and her pale green eyes matched the color of her dress almost perfectly. Her lips parted into a smile that revealed unnaturally white and straight teeth. She opened the door fully, came toward Andrew, and took his hand. Without saying a word, she pulled him into the room, which was completely bare except for a round bed and a mirror covering one of the walls. The lights were off, but moonlight coming through the window bounced off the mirror and provided enough light to see. The woman shut the door and led Andrew over to the bed, which resembled a giant aspirin. Finally, she spoke.

"I'm glad you came. I was getting lonely up here by myself."

"Why don't you join the party?"

"It's much lonelier to be around lots of people, don't you think?"

"Depends who the people are."

The woman waved her hand, sweeping away the concept of people.

"Oh, it doesn't matter," she said. "It's all just talk talk talk. No one says anything, really. Nothing with any meaning."

She walked over to the night table and took a small glass vial from the Kate Spade bag resting on it. She opened the vial, which had a tiny spoon attached to its cap.

"I like to share," she said, dipping the spoon into the vial and extracting a small amount of white powder from it. "I'll do it alone if I have to, but I find it extremely depressing."

"What is it?"

The woman began to giggle. She covered her mouth with her hand until she stopped.

"It's coke, silly. What planet are you from?"

She held the spoon beneath her nose, pinched her right nostril shut and inhaled the cocaine. She scooped some more and offered it to Andrew.

"I can't," Andrew said, leaning back from it.

"You can't or you won't?"

"I shouldn't. I never have."

The woman pouted.

"Why not?" she said, in a baby voice. "Just once."

Andrew looked around the room and his reflection in the mirrored wall startled him.

"What's your name?" he said.

"Simone."

"I'm Andrew Kane. Do you have a last name?"

Simone scowled at him.

"It doesn't matter, does it?" She softened a bit and offered the cocaine again. "I'll kiss you if you do it."

Andrew's eyes dropped to her lips: moist and pillowy, perfectly delineated by her red lipstick. He hadn't kissed a woman in quite some time and wondered if he even remembered how to. He breathed in her scent, like exotic flowers, then leaned down and snorted the cocaine into his left nostril, the same way she had. The drug coated the roof of his mouth and began to drip down the back of his throat. His tongue went numb and his heart began to flutter. It tasted bitter and medicinal. He looked in the mirrored wall again and watched himself wipe his nose.

"Where do you get this stuff?" he said.

"Do another."

Simone served up a fresh spoonful and Andrew took it into his right nostril this time. Then Simone kissed him and he drew her close, wrapping his arms around her waist and pushing his tongue into her mouth. He brought his hands up to her cheeks, but Simone pulled away when the door opened behind them.

"I see you've met the lady of the house," Jack said, standing in the entrance, his arm around Gwendolyn Pavlik. They stepped into the room and closed the door. "This is Gwendolyn, Andrew. Sorry I didn't introduce you before."

Gwendolyn extended her hand, but exerted only a weak grip when Andrew took it.

"You're the fisherman Jack's been telling me about," she said, her voice straining through what sounded like a perpetual state of boredom. "I've never met a real fisherman before."

"We're not very interesting, really."

"Who is interesting?" Gwendolyn began to circle Andrew, inspecting him from all sides. She came up behind him and sniffed the back of his neck. "You smell like the sea."

"Sorry. I didn't get a chance to shower."

"I'm glad you didn't." Gwendolyn circled back in front of Andrew and took his hands in hers. "They feel like leather," she purred, rubbing her thumbs across his callused palms. "I like leather." And with animal-like quickness, she lunged at Andrew and bit into his throat. Her teeth closed around his windpipe and she circled her tongue over his Adam's apple. She released her bite. "You taste good, Andrew."

"Thank you," Andrew said, rubbing his throat.

"Are you in love with me, now?"

"How could I be in love with you?"

"Every man falls in love with me. It's so fucking tedious."

Jack took a hit of Simone's cocaine, then went over to the window and looked out at the moon.

"There you have it, Andrew," he said, speaking to the view. "Beautiful women are bored. What's the world coming to when beautiful women are bored?"

He returned to the bed, where Simone was sitting. He looked down at her, as if trying to decide her fate. Then he reached toward her, a tender gesture, perhaps to stroke her hair or caress her cheek. He slapped the vial from her hand instead. It flew through the air and shattered against the mirror, dusting the carpet with cocaine and bits of glass.

"Please come to the window with me, Simone," he said, smiling down at the startled woman.

"Why?"

"Don't ask questions. That's not your purpose."

He pulled Simone to her feet and led her over to the window, where he pushed down on her shoulders, forcing her to her knees before him.

"I want you to help me enjoy this beautiful moon, Simone," he said. "If you don't mind."

"I don't understand."

"Don't play dumb, you pretty little whore."

Gwendolyn sat on the bed and patted the mattress.

"Come here, Andrew. Come sit with me."

Andrew sat next to her. He heard Jack's zipper being undone behind him.

"That's right," Jack cooed. "That's a good, good girl."

Gwendolyn began to massage the back of Andrew's neck, digging her nails into his skin. She leaned close to him and took his earlobe between her front teeth. Andrew heard Simone begin to moan softly and Jack start to grunt. Gwendolyn released his ear.

"Do you like my movies, Andrew?"

"I don't know if I've seen any."

"What about *Autumn Curse*?"

"Oh, yeah. I liked that one."

Gwendolyn slapped the back of Andrew's hand, lightly.

"Don't lie to me," she said.

"I'm not lying. I thought it was good."

Gwendolyn made a sour face.

"I think it was awful. Tell me what you catch."

"Fish . . . mostly."

"Big ones?"

"I try to."

"I like big fish."

The sounds coming from the window grew louder.

"Jack's an animal," Gwendolyn said.

"I can see that."

Then Jack let out a long, slow groan that evolved into a whoop and a laugh.

"Tropper, my man, it looks like you have to keep your fish on a tighter line," he said, zipping up.

He left Simone on her knees by the window and came back to the bed, a smile on his face.

"Let's go get some champagne, Andy," he said. "Before they drink it all."

CHAPTER
4

Jack hit the brakes and the tires of his Porsche squealed against the tarmac. The car stopped only inches from the wooden barrier separating the parking lot from Indian Wells Beach.

"I thought fishermen were supposed to be brave," he said, amused by the fear lingering on Andrew's face.

"There's a difference between brave and stupid," Andrew said, releasing his grip on the dashboard.

Jack turned off the engine and got out of the car with the bottle of champagne he'd taken from Tropper's party. Andrew and Gwendolyn got out, too. They followed Jack onto the beach, a wide, flat one with fine, cream-colored sand. The stars shone dully through the humidity and the surf pounded even intervals, white flashes of foam breaking the darkness. Andrew could see the lights of the shore-front houses, and he could hear laughter and singing coming from the people gathering around bonfires dotting the beach in either direction.

Gwendolyn took off her high heels and caught up to Jack, spraying sand back as she ran. Andrew thought she looked like a little girl running. He saw her ghostly figure jump on Jack's back and wrap her thin arms around his shoulders.

"Hurry up, Andrew!" she called out.

They were headed toward a deserted fire burning a few hundred yards down the beach, and as they walked, it occurred to Andrew that years had passed since he'd been here. He remembered learning about Indian Wells Beach in school, how the Montauket Indians drank from the spring here. Of course, now the Indians are long gone and the spring is dry. Only the beach bearing its name remains. He kept walking and memories began to return, slowly at first, then rapidly. The one with Katie stood out most vividly.

Senior prom tradition dictated watching the sunrise from Indian Wells after the big night. Most of the class went, and after getting his date home before her curfew, Andrew did as well. Katie and her date had argued about something at the dance, so she came to the beach alone. And there, on a spot not far from where Andrew stood now, they had sat together, watching the horizon lighten, drinking beer from long-necked bottles. Andrew couldn't remember everything they talked about that morning, but he did remember Katie turning to him at one point.

"I'm going to miss you, Andrew."

"I'll be back from time to time."

"No you won't. No one ever comes back once they leave here."

Katie was talking about the baseball scholarship. Almost every pitching record at East Hampton High had belonged to Andrew then. Most still stood. The University of Arizona had offered a free education in exchange for his arm and Andrew took it. He left in the fall and pitched against some of the country's best college players that spring. It was his first time away from home, and at times, he did wonder if he'd ever want to return to Long Island. Word of his fastball and his slider spread quickly, and pro scouts as well as pretty coeds began to attend his games. He didn't lose all season, and talk was he wouldn't last the full four years before the majors beckoned with money he couldn't refuse.

It didn't happen that way, though. No one, least of all Andrew, expected his father to die of a heart attack that summer, in the water, hauling net. One of the last haul-seine fishermen on the East End of Long Island, Charles Kane and his crew would push his dory out through the ocean waves each morning, lay net, then drag it back; the kind of work that ages a man and keeps him young at the same time. It was a hard life, but Charles Kane always said he wouldn't want to live any other.

Andrew tried to land a position pitching in the minors after his father died. But he found he couldn't concentrate anymore, not enough to place the ball where he needed to. How could he think about pitching when he had a kid sister to support and a mother who had developed breast cancer? So he took over his father's dory and crew, and when he could get a loan from the bank, he gave up haul-seining and bought a 40-foot trawler. He named it *Bessie*, after his mother. Some years on the water were good and some were bad, but as they passed, Andrew's right arm became better at pulling nets and wrestling clam rakes than throwing baseballs. Out on the water and at the bar, he would sometimes think about what might have been, but mostly he thought about the fish, and how to find them.

On that post-prom morning, with the future still spread out wide before them, he and Katie watched the sun climb and color the sky. The rest of the class had broken off into twos by then. Andrew finished his beer and pushed the empty bottle into the sand. He had wanted to kiss Katie since that day in eighth grade. The desire had been building steadily. But he couldn't find the nerve to that morning, or the right words.

"Don't worry, Katie," he said. "I'll be back."

The fire they came to burned silently, giving off no crackle or pop, no sparks flying off into the night. Its flames hardly moved despite the steady onshore breeze. If it had belonged to anyone earlier, they had left no evidence of having been there.

"I wonder whose it is," Gwendolyn said.

"It's ours now." Jack shrugged her off his back and pushed a piece of driftwood into the flames with his foot. He turned to Andrew. "You know why people like fire? It's the death urge. Booze and drugs and wars and fucking without condoms. It's all the same thing."

He drank some champagne straight from the bottle and began to sing into the neck:

"*. . . The summer wind came blowin' in from across the sea. It lingered there to touch your hair and walk with me.*"

His voice sounded smooth, almost professional, and he started to dance as he sang.

"*All summer long we sang a song and strolled that golden sand. Two sweethearts and the summer wind . . . .*"

Gwendolyn joined him and they moved around the fire, dangerously close to the flames.

"Dance with her, Andrew," Jack said, after a few minutes.

"That's okay. I'm a bit tired."

"Step up to the plate, fisher boy. Be a man."

Andrew took some of Jack's champagne first, then joined Gwendolyn. Jack sat in the sand and started to hum a strange, haunting tune. Andrew put his hands on Gwendolyn's waist and she began to sway her hips and slowly shimmy her shoulders. He followed her lead and soon found a rhythm. He didn't feel self-conscious dancing, like he normally did. The champagne was taking care of that. Gwendolyn narrowed her eyes and locked them on his. She thrust her pelvis and Andrew began to harden. Gwendolyn pushed herself against it even more.

Jack stopped humming, but they kept dancing and soon Andrew heard voices coming from somewhere down the beach. The voices grew louder and stronger until two teenaged girls, one blonde, one brunette, stepped into the ring of firelight. Their mouths dropped open when they saw Jack sitting there.

"That's right, girls. I'm Jack Hawker," Jack said. "Don't have an orgasm yet." He pointed across the fire at Gwendolyn and Andrew. "That's Gwendolyn Pavlik. You've seen her movies, too. The guy with her is Andrew Kane. He's a nobody. You've probably never seen him before in your life."

"Oh my god!" the blonde said.

"Close, but not quite," Jack said. "Have some champagne, ladies. You look way underage, but what the hell."

Jack handed the bottle to the blonde. She took a sip and passed it to her friend, who drank, too, and wrinkled her nose.

"Don't you like champagne, darling?" Gwendolyn said to her.

"I like wine coolers," the brunette answered.

"If I'd known, I would have brought a six-pack of Bartles and Jaymes," Jack said. "Sit down. Stay awhile."

The girls looked at each other again. The blonde giggled and the brunette gave a "Why not?" shrug.

They sat on either side of Jack and he kept the bottle passing back and forth between them. Andrew watched them from the other side of the fire, through a curtain of flames, wondering if he knew their parents.

"Are you girls in school?" Jack asked.

"We have another month before graduation," the brunette answered.

"Do you have jobs lined up yet?"

"Not yet."

"Well, I might be looking for an assistant. Would you be interested?"

"That would be totally awesome," both girls said, nearly in unison.

"The problem is I'm only going to need one." Jack passed the bottle to the brunette. "Champagne drinking would be a major requirement, of course. That and other things."

"I am so totally wasted," the blonde said.

"Me, too," said the brunette. "And I can't freaking believe

we're drinking champagne on the beach with Jack Hawker and Gwendolyn Pavlik. How cool is that?"

"And we're going to be his assistant."

"Not so fast," Jack said. "I told you I'll only need one. I'll have to decide which of you is best for the position."

"How are you going to do that?" the blonde asked, taking Jack's bait.

Jack pinched his chin between his thumb and index finger, pretending to ponder the question.

"I'm afraid I'll need to get a better look at you. Why don't both of you stand up?"

The girls did.

"Now, undress."

"Undress?" the brunette said.

"No need to be shy. I've done plenty of love scenes."

Neither girl moved at first. Jack clapped his hands together.

"What are you two waiting for? Puberty?"

The girls began to undress, looking neither at Jack nor at Gwendolyn and Andrew, nor at each other. Gwendolyn wolf whistled when they'd stripped down to their panties. Andrew averted his eyes, wanting to look but too embarrassed for the girls to do it.

"What's the matter, Andy boy?" Jack said, noticing Andrew's reticence.

"Nothing's the matter."

Jack stood between the girls.

"You know what morality is?" he said, looking through the fire at Andrew. "It's God's way of keeping everyone from having fun. And on that note, I'm going to take these nice girls for their interviews."

Jack draped his arms over each of the girl's shoulders, then steered them off into the night.

"You don't mind that he does that?" Andrew said to Gwendolyn, when they were gone.

Gwendolyn shrugged and began to run her hand up and down Andrew's back, her fingers tracing his vertebrae.

"Do you want to dance some more, Andrew?"

"Why don't we just sit here for a while?"

Gwendolyn began to nibble the side of his neck. It felt good and Andrew tilted his head to allow her better access. Then, suddenly, Gwendolyn pushed him back onto the sand, grabbed his wrists and pinned them down.

"What do you have to say about this, Andrew?" she said, straddling him, a triumphant look on her face.

"Say about what?" Andrew said, too tired to struggle or think of a more clever answer.

"You don't have a lot to say, do you?"

"Sometimes, I do."

"I bet mostly you're kind of the strong silent type. Who knows, maybe you're the dumb silent type."

Gwendolyn reached down and undid Andrew's pants. She pushed his jeans and underwear to his knees, then put him inside of her.

"Have you ever been fucked by a movie star?" she said, running her tongue over her upper lip, slowly grinding against him.

"What about Jack?" Andrew gasped.

"Jack will be fine. He can take care of himself."

Gwendolyn started to move faster on him. She began to rake his sides with her nails, drawing blood. But Andrew didn't feel the pain, only the pleasure. He stared up at her face and noticed that it looked more like a mask now than real. He almost came, but clenched it back until it passed. Gwendolyn leaned down and he thought she might kiss him. She began to lick circles around his eyes instead, tracing the sockets with her tongue. She then sucked on each one individually, as if trying to pull it into her mouth.

"You're mine now," she said, still riding him, still digging her nails into his sides. Andrew felt his groin begin to contract again, beyond his control this time. He came hard.

"That's it. Give it to me, fisherman."

Andrew didn't remember Gwendolyn climbing off of

him afterward. He didn't remember speaking to her, either, only her face above him fading with the remainder of his strength. He slept but woke later and found Gwendolyn still kneeling beside him, her hands poised to choke him now.

"Don't," he whispered, unable to speak any louder. "Don't."

He passed out again and woke hours later. Gwendolyn was gone and Jack stood over him now, the two girls at his side. The three of them were naked and both girls were staring off into the night, swaying ever so slightly, like trees in a breeze. The blonde held a pair of ripped panties. The brunette's hair looked pulled and tangled.

"Sleep tight, Andy boy," Jack said. "You had a rough day, didn't you?"

Andrew woke again at dawn and found the fire had burned out. He sat up, then stood and walked to the edge of the water. The breeze had died and the surf had gentled somewhat and his head ached. He took off his shirt and pants and placed them on the dry sand before wading into the water, the salt stinging where Gwendolyn had scratched him. The stinging soon subsided and he ducked under, hoping the cold might clear his head, or at least numb it a bit. He came up feeling a little better and swam out beyond the breakers. He turned parallel to the shore and began to breaststroke.

Dark, dense-looking clouds hung low over Napeague Bay. As Andrew swam, he noticed a triangular one that tapered down toward the water beneath it. He tired after swimming less than a hundred yards, and flipped onto his back. But instead of relaxing, he imagined something watching him from below. He thought of Seth Donahue, his head somewhere in the water with him, that gruesome hole where it should have been. He thought of Gwendolyn, too, her mask-like face, her hands poised to choke him. Did that really happen? He felt an inexplicable panic rise in his chest and he turned toward the beach and swam in.

He began to jog toward land when his feet touched bottom, still watching the triangular cloud. It had sharpened by now, and extended down into a spout, a gray column connecting the sky with the bay. It grew thicker and seemed to be moving closer. Andrew knew he couldn't escape if it stayed its course, trapped by the ocean behind him. The spout continued to grow and it darkened as it sucked the bay up into it. But the weight of the water it consumed slowed it and finally held it in place. A wave came from behind and knocked Andrew down. He got back to his feet and made his way onto the beach, where he continued watching the spout until it eventually broke apart and dissipated.

He dressed quickly and walked up to the parking lot, then along Indian Wells Road to the Montauk Highway. Only a few cars were on it, mainly fishermen heading to the docks and landscapers getting started before the heat built again. He stuck his thumb out, hoping to catch a ride as far east as Montauk village. He could walk home from there. He intended to sleep the rest of the day and not drink again at night. Several cars passed, one a convertible with a tuxedo-clad man standing on the passenger seat, his sunglasses on and a bottle of wine in his hand. He shouted something at Andrew as he sped past him.

Andrew started to walk, and a familiar red pickup pulled onto the shoulder less than a minute later. He jogged up to it and got in the passenger side.

"Don't ask," he said to Ralph, after shutting the door. "You wouldn't believe me anyway."

"You're probably right," Ralph said, giving Andrew a quizzical look before pulling back onto the road.

Andrew leaned up against the door and closed his eyes. He fell asleep well before they reached Montauk.

PART TWO

JUNE

The wintertime brings storms to the East End of Long Island. They drive waves high onto the ocean beaches, pitting them in a losing battle against the sea. The most powerful storms carve gullies in the ocean floor just offshore. The stone jetties built to protect the beaches often achieve just the opposite, allowing sand to build up in some places while speeding erosion in others.

By June, the heat is still welcome, still loosening muscles and joints clenched by the cold months. On this cusp of summer, the sky over the East End has a luminescent quality, its cotton-ball clouds softening and filtering the sun's rays. This shimmery light seems to linger longer than it should, reluctantly fading at the end of the day and allowing night to settle over the island.

In the fields, corn stalks have not yet reached the height of a man, and their ears are still small and tight. The tomatoes are green on the vine, no larger than golf balls. But these young crops give hope and a sense of expectation to the farmers, just as June does for the city people driving past their fields, headed to their summer houses for the first time all year.

For the young and single, the days that lay ahead inspire yearning for a new romance, one free of baggage and rancor, one defined by sunset strolls and star-lit kisses. To those city-bound all year, the coming days promise barbeques and swims and cocktails sipped on porsches overlooking the Atlantic. In June, hopes have not yet been sullied by too many traffic jams or bitter family conflicts or the realization that, once again, a summer in the Hamptons will probably bring no true happiness or transformation.

And out on the water, which is still too cold for all but

the hardiest human swimmers, the bluefish are beginning to run. They rove relentlessly, hunting and devouring anything and everything, even each other.

CHAPTER

5

Chad Jensen stood in front of the mirror and liked what he saw. I wouldn't change a thing, he thought. Like most people, Chad didn't see himself exactly the way others did. He didn't see that his face looked a little squished, the features somewhat crowded together, as if his mother's body had fought to keep him inside while giving birth to him. He also didn't think his unusually square head was unusually shaped at all. And he didn't realize that his slight cross-eye and his crooked smile gave him a menacing air which made most people he met a little uneasy. At least I have my looks, he thought, engaging himself in yet another protracted stare fight.

He dropped down and did fifty pushups. Have to keep the arms and pecs in good shape. He got up and stood in front of the mirror again, watching the blood from the exertion drain from his deeply tanned face. In truth, he hadn't been out in the sun all winter. No trips to the islands for him, or even a session at a tanning parlor. Bain De Soleil tanning cream did the trick without the risk of skin cancer or premature wrinkles. It was cheaper, too. Chad slapped some more cologne onto the back of his neck and checked to make sure his white cotton T-shirt, a size too small, hadn't stretched out any. Then he smiled, but not because he felt particularly happy. He considered it practice. All the movie stars had a signature smile, one they flashed with ease, a convincing smile no matter how shitty they felt at the moment.

Shitty. That was exactly how Chad had been feeling for some years now. And why not? Any normal person who considered himself good-looking, talented and charming would feel badly in his situation. In his mind, he just needed a chance, a break, someone to give him a hand. What bothered Chad particularly was that no one seemed to ever want to help him. Not anymore.

The pool house he was occupying for the summer belonged to Penny Baskin, wife of Francis Baskin, the famous movie director. Francis Baskin. Now there's a first class prick if I ever saw one, Chad thought. So he's had a few big hits. That doesn't mean his shit smells any better than mine. Kick the ladder out once you're on board. That's what they all do as soon as they make it. All I want is an opportunity to tell you about my project, Francis. A meeting's not too much to ask, is it? But will you give it to me? I'm sure you wouldn't. Why give your wife's personal trainer a meeting? He thought about the deal Penny had made. Is it worth it, Penny? The big mansion in the Hamptons, the duplex on Park Avenue, the trips to the South of France. I figure all that can get kind of dull if you're not getting the old high hard one once in a while. I guess that's where I come in.

Chad didn't like feeling so angry and resentful, but he couldn't help thinking about how things had turned out much differently than he'd planned. Like many aspiring actors, his dream had begun in a small town, as far from Hollywood as it was from the Hamptons. Lastrup, Minnesota offered few diversions besides the movies. Growing up, Chad had gone to see every one that came to the Cineplex, which was located in the mall that had put most of Lastrup's Main Street out of business.

Chad had joined the army after high school. He made a lousy soldier, though. He got into fine physical shape, but never learned to shoot a gun or take an order very well. He wasted no time moving to New York after his stint in the army. He found work bartending at The Tunnel on West 27th Street. Did he get laid? Sure he did. That's what New York club bartenders do. Did he get a swelled head about his looks and abilities? Of course. Everyone he worked with took acting lessons and went on auditions. Chad did, too. Before long, he landed a few parts, mainly in small Off- Off- Off-Broadway productions that called for a young, buff guy to mostly stand around being young and buff. Agents came to some of the plays, and one of them in particular had an idea about how Chad might best maximize his minimal acting talent. Dialogue had never been Chad's strong suit, so why not accentuate the physical? Welcome to pornography, Chad. There's always money to be made in porn, even if the agent takes a substantial cut. So that's where Chad ended up, working steadily as Johnny Love, the moniker his agent chose for him.

Chad lost track of how many Triple X movies he made over the course of six years. Because of all the cocaine and alcohol he consumed, he lost track of his money, as well. Eventually, the roles stopped coming. "No one wants to see the same fucking guy fucking year after year." That's how Chad explained his career downturn. "Fresh meat is the order of the day in today's porn industry," he would lament to the few people who cared to listen. "There's no loyalty anymore," he'd complain. "That's why you can't build a career in the industry like they did in the Seventies." His porn career in shambles, Chad went back to acting class, only to find that his once-meager skills had deteriorated beyond repair.

But one thing he still knew was fitness. Now he just had to figure out how to make money from it. So he got his trainer's certification and eventually found a job at the Edge

Gym on the Upper East Side. There he began to acquire clients, mostly women, many of them horny with rich husbands and lots of time. He began to train them privately and soon had a big enough client list to go out on his own. That's what he did, training them and fucking them in roughly equal measure. He soon began to narrow his list to those who would pay the most for both services. Penny Baskin happened to be one of them, and three years ago Chad had agreed to train her exclusively during the summers.

Chad paced back and forth across the small, one room pool house, then went back to the mirror.

"I am who you are," he said into it. "I am who you were and I am who you will be. Do you understand what I am telling you? You can't escape it. You can't run and you can't hide. Because I'll find you. You can't escape my love just like you can't escape death and taxes and your own desire and dreams and fucked up existence."

He practiced that monologue daily. He'd written it one night after drinking half a bottle of vodka. He planned to use it on auditions when he perfected it, and eventually expand it into a screenplay. He thought it was brilliant even though he had almost no idea what it meant. Good writing is supposed to be hard to understand, he thought. Good writing can't be explained. It wouldn't be any good if it could be. He hoped to turn the screenplay into a movie ultimately, but knew he needed money for that, the kind no one would readily give to him. The bastards. Well, they'll be knocking on my door some day, he thought. And it won't be the door of a pool house. That's for sure.

He tried not to think so negatively. After all, here he was, summering in the Hamptons. Most people would kill for that. No rent to pay. Not much work to do. An hour a day, at most. The rest of the time he could spend on the beach or walking around East Hampton or reading by the pool. But reading never interested him much, and looking at stores stocked with items too expensive to buy only annoyed him.

And the beach made him uneasy. He had never learned to swim back in landlocked Minnesota. But mainly he didn't like looking at the women in their bikinis. He found it too frustrating, yet not for the normal reason. He assumed he could have any girl he wanted. No difficulty there, he thought, given my looks and physique. The problem was that he didn't really want any of them, not anymore, not like he used to. He figured this was due to having had too many women—over three hundred, he estimated. He wondered if a guy could actually fuck all the desire and lust out of his system. He worried that might be the case with himself.

Not that he had any problem functioning. It had become almost automatic, part of his job. He still got hard, just never very aroused. But hard was all he needed to keep his clients coming back for more. Hard paid the bills and allowed him to spend summers in East Hampton each year, for what it was worth. Still, he worried that this automatic ability might fail him one day—followed by his looks. Then what?

Chad resumed pacing, then stopped and looked in the mirror once again. He frowned, but only for a moment. Can't let wrinkles grow. I need a plan, he thought. A plan, a plan, a plan. He went over to the bed, stretched out on it and tried to think of one. He jerked off instead, out of habit rather than any real desire to. It took a while and the only fantasy he could conjure was the usual one with the faceless woman in bondage gear, bound and gagged and whimpering. In it, he always forced her to serve as his footrest while he watched TV in an easy chair. He'd been using that fantasy a lot lately.

He lay there for a while after he finished, his semen cooling on his stomach. Then he got up and cleaned it off. He didn't feel any better now or more relaxed. If anything, he felt more anxious and depressed. He looked out the window and saw the two little Baskin kids in the pool. Chad didn't like most kids. These ones he hated, mainly because they hated him, too. The mid-day sun served as a further deterrent to his going out. Sunny days always reminded him that he should be happy and enjoying himself, even though he had no idea how to.

So he sat on the edge of the bed and tried to think, to find a way to turn his life around. It was all about money. He had that part figured out. The question that remained: how to get it, enough to make his movie. He buried his face in his hands and closed his eyes. He also pushed his ears shut to blot out the Baskin kids, who had begun to scream at each other. A plan, a plan, a plan. Money, money, money. Fame, fortune, the power to say fuck you to anybody and everybody. You're right in the middle of it, Chad. Just find a way to take it. I deserve it, don't I? Why not me? I've paid my dues. Okay, calm down, Chad. Calm down and think.

CHAPTER 6

Andrew's house looked much like that of any other Montauk fisherman; small, one-story, covered with faded red tar shingles. The back yard had accumulated a sizable collection over the years: gill nets and clam rakes and lobster traps and salt-crusted buoys. Nothing about the inside would surprise anyone who saw the outside first. A fresh coat of paint would help brighten the neat but neglected interior. So would new furniture and rugs to replace what had been serving Andrew for more years than he could remember.

He woke and found Jack sitting in the chair across from his bed. He hadn't seen Jack in over a week, since the night of Dean Tropper's party.

"How the hell did you get in here, Jack?"

"Through the door. How else?"

"I always lock it."

"Not this time."

Andrew tried to recall locking it, but couldn't. It occurred to him that he'd never given Jack his address.

"Hang on a minute. How did you know where I live?"

"I looked you up in the phone book, idiot. Now, get out of bed. I've got things for us to do today."

Andrew swung his feet over the side of the bed. He felt silly sitting there in only his underpants. He also felt tired and hung over from too many beers at Moran's.

"You have fun the other night?" Jack said.

"Did you?"

"I detect some judgment in your tone."

"I don't think those girls were even legal."

"So, arrest me, officer."

"You do that kind of thing all the time?"

Jack grinned.

"Wouldn't you?"

"I don't know."

"Of course, you don't. You've never had the opportunity. Take a shower."

Andrew didn't make any move toward the bathroom. He didn't like being ordered around in his own house, especially by someone who hadn't been invited.

"How's Gwendolyn?" he asked, unsure what else to say.

"You'd know as well as me," Jack said, eyeing the scabbed-over scratches on Andrew's torso. He stood and went over to the picture of Andrew's kids hanging in the wall.

"These yours?"

"Yep."

"How old are they?"

"Charlie's six. Annie's three."

"Cute little buggers."

"You have any yourself?"

"Probably. Now get your ass in the shower. And don't forget to brush your teeth. Your breath smells like you've been eating dog shit."

Francis Baskin's mansion on Further Lane had once belonged to the Foster family, whose ancestors had stepped off the Mayflower and immediately started converting Long

Island's once dense, hardwood forests into lumber. Successive Foster generations had gone into boat building, then whaling, then shipping. Francis Baskin liked living in a piece of American history, especially since his own line in this country didn't extend back very far. Bascinowitz had become Baskin some time after his great grandfather made it off Ellis Island. He'd bought the mansion after the success of *American Death*, and had built a new wing and the pool house after making the equally successful *Commando IV*. He didn't actually need more space and he hated pools, but it seemed like the Hampton thing to do.

Francis answered the door as soon as Jack rang his bell. He was dressed in Bermuda shorts and a green polo shirt that accentuated his carefully maintained physique. He shook Jack's hand and his smile deepened the creases in his lean, tanned, clean-shaven cheeks.

"Sorry I didn't see you at Tropper's Memorial Day party, Jack," he said, his deep voice almost a parody of manliness. "I was on a conference call with that bastard Trent Krueger and that prick Harry Whiner. It lasted half the night."

"Don't worry. You didn't miss anything. Francis, this is Andrew Kane. He's a fisherman."

Francis shook Andrew's hand with a grip that matched the strong set of his jaw.

"Pleased to meet you, Andrew. I assume you're going to teach Jack all about your trade."

"I'll try my best."

They took Jack's Porsche. Jack had put the top down and he drove fast along Further Lane, working the shift around every curve and at the base of each rise. He tailgated slower cars and passed them at the slightest opportunity. He pulled up behind a pickup truck loaded with lawnmowers and gardening tools. He leaned on the horn until it pulled onto the shoulder.

"Fucker shouldn't be allowed on the roads," he grumbled, accelerating past it.

As they passed the Maidenstone Club golf course, a golf ball bounced on the road in front of them. Jack barely slowed turning onto Route 114, which snaked through woods that hid the houses of those who couldn't afford property closer to the beach. He finally slowed when he came into Sag Harbor. Route 114 ended at the waterfront and Jack turned right toward the yacht club. He parked there and pointed to his boat, a sleek fiberglass craft with radar and sonar equipment on its bridge, a glassed-in bow deck, and two stern decks. "Diablo" was painted on the hull in an arc of gold letters.

"There's my baby," he said.

He led the way up the gangplank and to the upper stern deck, where they settled into mounted swivel seats. Andrew noticed that *Diablo's* lower stern deck featured two mounted fighting chairs, fitted with gimbals for the butt of a rod. He noticed ginpoles for hauling large fish slanting off the port and the starboard sides.

"Take us out for awhile," Jack said into an intercom built into the armrest of his seat. He turned to Andrew. "I see you noticed my hobby."

"Sport fishing."

"For sharks, mainly."

The engines grumbled to life and *Diablo* backed out of her slip. She turned around, then slowly motored out of the harbor, cruising past folks fishing from the long, paved jetty that served as a town parking lot. Some of the fishermen waved. Only Andrew waved back. *Diablo* headed east around Barcelona Point and across Northwest Harbor. It passed Cedar Point on its way into Gardiner's Bay, which is enclosed by the South Fork, Shelter Island and the North Fork on the other side. The water was calm today and the boat glided effortlessly through it.

"You want a drink, Francis?" Jack asked.

"J&B on the rocks. A triple, if you don't mind."

"How about you, Andrew?"

"Just a beer."

Through the intercom, Jack ordered the J&B for Francis,

a Budweiser for Andrew, and a Jamesons for himself. A crew-man dressed in shorts and a "Diablo" t-shirt brought the drinks. He returned a few minutes later with a plate of pani-ni sandwiches. Jack selected one filled with prosciutto, mari-nated mozzarella and roasted red peppers. He took a bite and washed it down with whiskey.

"Help yourselves, guys," he said.

Andrew took a sandwich, this one filled with lemon grilled chicken and marinated eggplant. It tasted better than any he'd ever eaten.

"You have a nice boat here, Jack," he said.

"Glad you like it. You'll have to come aboard again."

Francis drank a large swallow of J&B and looked out at Shelter Island. The boat was skirting its eastern edge, heading into the Peconic Bay.

"What do you think, Francis?" Jack said.

Francis didn't answer at first. He had switched his gaze to the captain on the bridge, a handsome, dark-haired man.

"Think about what?" he said, finally, still looking at the captain.

"We'll need someone to replace Seth, the poor bastard."

Francis laughed and looked at Jack.

"I've heard of actors trying to weasel out of contracts, but Seth really went all the way, didn't he?"

"He must have a good agent," Jack said. "By the way, Allen Balford begged me to put a good word in for him. He's dying for the part."

"What's your good word?"

"Fuck him. That's my good word."

They cleared Shelter Island and headed into the Peconic. The water became choppy here and *Diablo* began to rock a little. Jack finished his whiskey and ordered another round. The drinks came and Francis ate some of a panino.

"Who do you have in mind?" he said to Jack.

"My instinct is we should get an unknown, a nobody who won't distract from the story."

Francis patted his mouth with a napkin.

"I agree. One star's enough."

"So maybe it's a good thing Seth died."

Their eyes met and they exchanged a grin. Francis gulped more scotch and Jack seemed to remember something important. He pulled a piece of paper from his back pocket and handed it to Andrew, who had been looking out at the water, trying not to listen to their conversation.

"What's this?" Andrew said, taking the paper.

"Some lines from the *Hamptons* script. Do me a favor and read them to me."

Andrew looked at the lines.

"Why do you want me to read this?"

"Just do it."

Andrew usually felt embarrassed reading out loud in front of people, even bedtime stories to Charlie and Annie. He began to read the lines.

"'I'm your man, Mary.'" He said the words slowly, woodenly. "'No matter what happens, I'm your man. I'll take care of you and the boy until the day I die. I promise, Mary. I promise, I will.'"

"Not bad," Jack said. "Read it again."

Andrew repeated the lines, more fluidly this time.

"Not bad at all," Francis said, his face beginning to flush, his eyes a bit loose in their sockets now.

"I think our Andrew here might have a future in acting," Jack said.

"You're kidding, right?" Andrew said.

"This whole business is a joke. Believe me."

"A complete joke," Francis added. "The only problem is, nobody's laughing." He swallowed more scotch, then slumped down in his seat, his legs splayed out in front of him. He burped. "Excuse me. I get a little seasick sometimes. The scotch doesn't help."

He finished his drink in this position and Andrew noticed his eyes becoming more watery and glazed. Francis grabbed onto his armrest to steady himself against the boats rocking. He burped again, then let his chin drop onto his chest. He stayed like that for a minute before lifting his chin again.

"I'm a fucking failure," he said, but in a flaccid voice that sounded like someone else's, not his own. "A complete and total and utter fucking failure." He looked at Andrew and smiled, as if suddenly remembering some distant pleasure. "You have nice eyes, fisherman."

"Thanks," Andrew said, somewhat taken aback, not sure how else to respond to the compliment.

"Don't thank me," Francis said. "Thank your parents. Or thank God or whoever gave them to you. Maybe the milkman. I don't know."

Jack leaned over and gave Francis a kiss on the cheek.

"That's what I love about you, Francis. All it takes is a couple drinks and a boat ride to wash the starch out of your shorts."

Francis smiled, weakly.

"I don't like starch in my shorts," he whined. "Very uncomfortable. Kiss me again, Jack. On the mouth."

"Francis!" Jack said, with mock horror. "What's gotten into you?"

"If you weren't the producer, Jack, I would insist on it. I would demand it." Francis's voice had gone several octaves.

"Sorry, Francis. Not me. But maybe Andrew will oblige you."

Andrew considered jumping over the side and swimming to shore—anything to escape this. *Diablo* cruised due east now, parallel to East Marion on the North Fork. Jack ordered another scotch for Francis. Francis held it up when it arrived, a toasting gesture.

"I want this to be the best movie I've ever made, Jack. You know why?"

"Why?"

"Because I want to be loved. That's why. Loved. Do you understand?"

"And why shouldn't you be?"

"If I make a good movie, people will admire me like they do Scorcese and Coppola and Truffaut. I want to be admired and loved and cherished all at the same time."

Francis sank further into his seat and started on his third J&B. Andrew didn't want to look at him anymore, but couldn't help it. Everything about the man had changed so suddenly. Even his taut muscles looked softer now, less defined.

"Don't worry, Francis," Jack said. "We'll make a good movie."

"Yes, we will, won't we? A very good movie."

Francis then closed his eyes and Jack took the scotch from his hand. He drank some of it and cringed.

"I don't know how he drinks this blended shit."

"He probably shouldn't drink at all," Andrew said.

"He needs to. Poor fucker would explode if he didn't."

Francis stirred and his eyes opened half-way, then shut again, for good. Jack stood and went to the railing. He leaned against it and looked down into the water.

"Is the fishing good here, Andrew?"

"Not very."

"Where is it good?"

"Depends what time of day and what time of year. Depends on the currents, too."

Jack turned around and faced Andrew. His eyes looked especially dark now, shadows cast by the early afternoon sun collected in the sockets.

"You found Seth's body, didn't you?" he said.

"What makes you say that?"

"They said on the radio a fisherman found him and you practically turned green when Tropper mentioned it at his party. Just a hunch."

Andrew sipped his beer, warm and mostly flat now.

"Yeah, I found him," he said.

"A shark, huh?"

"I'm not so sure."

"What do you think?"

"I don't know. No one does yet."

Jack turned around again and pointed east toward Greenport and Orient Point beyond it.

"How about over there? Any fish over there?"

Andrew looked out to where Jack had pointed.

"Sometimes you get blues and porgies. Sometimes you don't get anything."

"I guess that's the chance you take."

Andrew pictured Seth Donahue's body again. He experienced a wave of nausea as he imagined being sucked into the hole where the head had once been. That image stayed with him for the rest of the ride.

CHAPTER 7

Karla Sands pulled into the parking lot of the East Hampton Bank at 9:45pm. The lot was situated behind the bank, hidden from the Montauk Highway. Only a few cars were in it and the bank itself stood on the relatively remote stretch of highway between East Hampton and Amagansett. Still, Karla took the extra precaution of parking her BMW in the back of the lot, in the shadow of a large oak tree.

She opened the window, then turned off the engine and checked her watch.

"He better not be late, Furball," she said to the dog slumbering on the passenger seat. "If he is, Mommy Goddess will cut his fucking nuts off." Furball woke briefly and licked Karla's hand. "That's sweet of you, Furball. Why can't everyone be sweet like you and me?"

Crickets were chirping outside and a light breeze rustled the leaves of the oak tree. The air smelled of the sea and, between the sounds of cars passing on the highway, the surf could be heard grumbling in the distance. But Karla didn't notice any of this. The drab brick exterior of the bank had reminded her of Munsey, NY, and the working-class neighborhood she grew up in there. She wondered what the town looked like now, if it had changed much since she left. In her memories of the place, the sky was always gray, and it was always winter. She hadn't gone back much since graduating high school, and she wondered what had happened to the kids who used to call her Karla Sandwich because she was always the fattest girl in the class. She hoped *they* were all fat now, and poor, too.

She pushed Munsey from her mind, took out her mini-recorder and pressed the "Record" button:

"Another summer season has begun, students," she spoke into it. "And this one promises to be hotter than ever. Forget about New York for the next three months. The Hamptons are where it's happening and that's where everyone was Memorial Day weekend. Dean and Simone Tropper kicked off the season with their usual flair for the extravagant, opening their mansion and their hearts, treating us to the kind of party only they can throw. Who was there? The question, students, is who wasn't? And no time was wasted in getting into the scandalous spirit of the summer. Should I tell you? I don't know if I should. Okay, I will."

Karla bit her lower lip, concerned that she didn't actually have anything very interesting or scandalous to fill this month's column with. So far, she had nothing except for the usual rundown of who was there and what they wore. Not enough dirt for her readers. I certainly have spoiled the shit out of them, haven't I? she thought. They don't deserve me.

A battered old Ford Escort wheeled into the lot, its headlights glaring into Karla's eyes. She left the recorder on and put it in her bag. The Escort slowly toured the perimeter of the lot and stopped beside her. Marcus got out of it and Furball began to bark.

"Shut up, asshole!" Karla said, giving Furball a head spank. "Are you trying to blow it for me? Are you trying to ruin my career, you jealous little ingrate?"

Furball stopped barking and Marcus approached Karla's window.

"Fancy meeting you here, Karla."

"Oh, knock it off."

Marcus went around to the passenger side and nearly sat on Furball getting in.

Furball snapped at his ass and Karla grabbed the terrier's scruff and put her in the back seat.

"You can bite him afterward, Furball," she said. "Right now we have business."

Furball lay down on the back seat and curled into the fetal position.

"Nice dog," Marcus said, the combination of his cologne and personal odor almost causing Karla to gag.

"Thank you. She takes after her mommy, I like to think."

Marcus wagged his meaty index finger at Karla.

"You see, Karla. I knew you would make a good mother."

"Right now I have to give birth to this month's column. What do you have for me?"

Marcus felt for the recline lever along the side of his seat. He pulled it and the seat went back. He meshed his fingers across his stomach.

"This is a very comfortable car," he said.

"It's a sixty thousand dollar BMW. It better be comfortable."

"One day maybe I'll buy one. Actually, I like Mercedes better, but a BMW would do."

A Mercedes? Even that piece-of-crap Ford is too good for a slob like you, Karla thought. Don't say it, Karla. Hold your tongue. He's the best source you have right now.

"I can see you driving something even more glamorous," she said. "A Lamborghini or an Aston Martin, like James Bond."

"James Bond, huh?"

"Why not?"

Dream on, Karla thought. Now give me the goods and get the fuck out of my car before it has to be fumigated.

Marcus put his hands behind his head, as if preparing to take a nap. He yawned.

"It's nice out tonight, isn't it, Karla?"

"It's a bit humid for my taste."

"But it's peaceful." He turned his entire body toward Karla. "You know what I do when I have a night off like this? I go for a long walk on the beach."

"That's great, Marcus."

"I wait until very late and I walk in the dark, sometimes all the way to Montauk."

"That's a long way."

"Sometimes I take a taxi back. But what I like is that in the dark, I can't recognize anyone I pass and they can't recognize me. It's very nice. I look at the moon and the stars. I smell the ocean and feel the sand between my toes."

Karla couldn't help rolling her eyes.

"Sounds real spiritual," she said. "Now—"

"You know, Karla, it might seem silly, but when I walk, I like to imagine I'm back in Indian times, before the white men came here. It must have been beautiful then."

"I'm sure it was extremely beautiful, and extremely dull, too." Karla dared a look at Marcus. His eyes were closed now. "Don't fall asleep on me, Marcus. This isn't nap time."

Marcus opened his eyes, but stayed in a reclined, sideways position. His smile contained a hint of resignation.

"No, this isn't nap time at all," he said. "This is all business. Business, business, business . . ." His voice trailed off.

Karla looked straight ahead again, through the windshield at the drive-thru ATM attached to the bank. He seems even needier this summer, she thought, if that's possible.

"Marcus, you called *me*."

Marcus opened his eyes.

"Yes, I did."

"So, I assume you have something. If you do, please give it to me and I'll be happy to pay you for it. If you don't, then we can conclude this little meeting and you can go take a walk on the beach or pray to the moon or whatever else you do on your nights off."

"Oh, I have something good, Karla. But I was thinking that before I give it to you, maybe we can discuss our arrangement."

"I thought we already did."

"We did, but—"

"But what?"

"But maybe there's a way that's better for both of us."

Karla did two yoga breaths.

"Tell me what you want," she said. "I don't have time for games."

Marcus brought his hands from behind his head and put them on his stomach again. He slid them down toward the waistband of his jeans.

"You know, my wife left me this winter, Karla."

"That's too bad. I feel for you. I really do."

"Thank you, Karla. It's been tough. Very tough." Marcus used his thumb nail to pick a bit of broccoli from between his two front teeth. "It's been frustrating, too. Sometimes I get frustrated."

Karla considered starting the car and driving away. But what good would that do with Marcus still in it? She remembered telling him he was sexy the other night, and regretted putting that false idea in his head.

"What do you want from me, Marcus?"

Marcus slipped his fingers beneath his waistband. He undid the top button and smiled sheepishly at Karla. Karla smiled back but couldn't maintain it for long. She reached between Marcus's legs, slowly, seductively, then grabbed his balls and squeezed them hard.

"Okay, limpdick, no more game playing," she said. "I wouldn't suck your hairy little penis for all the good dirt in the world. You got that? Do you understand?"

Marcus nodded, his eyes wide with a combination of amazement and pain. Karla squeezed his balls even harder.

"I'm glad we're on the same page," she said. "Now, what do you have for me? Tell me or I'll crack your balls like walnuts."

"Okay! Okay! Just let go first."

Karla released Marcus and almost laughed at the agony twisting his face.

"Out with it, Marcus. I don't have all night."

"All right! All right! Simone Tropper. She's messing around behind Dean's back."

"How do you know? What's your source?"

"Someone at the party. I can't tell you her name, but I trust her. She was out on the lawn, and when she looked up at the house, she saw Simone in a second floor window with Jack Hawker."

Marcus paused to maximize the power he'd regained.

"What were they doing?" Karla said, making no effort to conceal her impatience with this tactic.

"Simone was giving him a blow job, right there in the window."

"I guess some guys have all the luck, huh, Marcus? And here I thought Dean and Simone had the perfect marriage, a real love match. Anything else?"

"Karla, that's pretty good, I think."

"If it's true."

"It is."

"Promise?"

"Yes, I promise."

Marcus flinched when Karla reached for her bag. She took her purse from it, and from the purse, she took two hundred-dollar bills. She handed them to Marcus, who immediately reached for the door handle.

"Did I hurt you, Marcus?" Karla said, her voice all sugary now.

"I'll be okay."

"You know, you're right. It *is* a nice night."

Marcus nodded, then got out and limped over to his Escort. Karla reached into the back seat and nudged Furball awake.

"Mommy Goddess did very well tonight, Furball. You

would have been proud of me if you'd been courteous enough to stay awake."

Marcus started his Escort and pulled away. He stopped at the drive-thru ATM and Karla watched him insert his bank card and deposit the money she'd paid him. She watched him take his receipt and drive off, then took the recorder from her bag and spoke into it:

"Okay, students, here's a quiz for you. Which very successful real estate man, whom you all know, can't seem to keep his pretty young wife satisfied? Here are some clues: Short man, tall buildings. East Hampton mansion, lavish parties. Enter dashing action/adventure star and let's just say some action took place upstairs while hubby hosted downstairs. Still don't know? Well, I'm not going to tell. That wouldn't be right now, would it?"

Karla stopped the recorder and looked back at Furball.

"It's going to be a good column, Furball." She picked up the terrier and kissed her dark, thin lips. "What do you think?"

CHAPTER 8

This afternoon, Chad listened to Penny even less than he usually did. It was always the same thing coming out of her mouth, mainly complaints about problems most people would give their right arm to have. But to be fair, Chad did feel a little sorry for her.

Anyone who didn't know better might think Penny had a perfect life, married to a rich and famous director, living in an East Hampton mansion in the summer and on Park Avenue during the rest of the year. Not bad for a poor girl from Flatbush—especially one who isn't very pretty, at least not according to most men. She'd met Francis when he was shooting a scene from *Urban Warrior* on her block in Brooklyn. Penny was an extra for a few days. Not until several years after they married did she find out the truth about him.

Chad sat on the edge of the bed while Penny rode the stationary bike in her light blue Danskin. He watched *The Young and the Restless* on the TV, every once in a while looking over at Penny to make sure she didn't pedal any slower than she already was.

"Do I have to go for half an hour, Chad?"

"You don't have to do anything you don't want."

Penny hadn't even broken a sweat. A certain amount of effort must be exerted to break a sweat.

"Chad, I'm feeling tight. I think it's from the dumbbells yesterday."

"They were only two-pounders."

"I know. But I need a massage."

"You need to break a sweat first. I'll massage you if you break a sweat."

"No. Now. Massage me now."

"All right. Just keep riding the bike. I'll massage you while you ride."

Chad didn't really care if she stayed in shape or not. He got off the bed, went over to Penny and began massaging her shoulders. Penny rolled her neck.

"Oh, that feels nice."

"Good. Keep pedaling."

Chad dug his fingers into her shoulder muscles. He stood behind her while he did it. This gave him the opportunity to look around her spacious bedroom and plan where to put the video camera. It had to be a spot where she wouldn't notice it, but one with a clear, unobscured shot of the bed. He scanned the built-in bookcase and her art deco dresser. Nothing suitable there. The windowsill would be way too exposed. Beneath the neon pink love seat would be too low. His eyes darted around and finally came to rest on the hanging plant, a big, bushy wandering Jew, its vine-like leaves stretching nearly to the floor. Perfect. The camera could rest right inside it, hidden in its own little jungle.

"Do you like training me, Chad?"

Chad kept massaging.

"Sure, I do," he said.

"How do I compare to your other clients?"

"What do you mean?"

"Am I as good as them?"

"Absolutely."

"But do you like me better?"

Chad took a moment to think of an answer. He didn't really dislike Penny, but then, he didn't particularly like her. He didn't admire her, yet he didn't despise her, either. Neutral bordering on mild contempt would be the most accurate description of how he felt about her. This would work to his favor; no sentiment or conscience getting in his way.

"I do like you better than my other clients," he fibbed. "Why do you think I come out here?"

Chad eyed the hanging plant again and decided he'd have to buy a small camera, one that didn't weigh very much.

"I'm getting tired," Penny said.

"You just started."

"Do I have to do crunches today?"

"I'll think of something else for you to do."

Penny kept pedaling and Chad continued to massage her. He felt her shoulders begin to relax.

"I wish I could have you massaging me all the time, Chad. I get so tense. I don't know why."

"You should just relax."

"I try to, but whenever I leave the house, there's always something that upsets me. Like just yesterday, I was in the Shoeless Princess and this rude woman cuts right in front of me on the line. I mean, I'm standing there waiting to pay for my baguette and this woman just steps right in front of me."

"What did you do?" Chad said, yawning.

"I gave her a piece of my mind. That's what I did. The nerve of her. The problem is everyone's discovered the Hamptons. Now you can't even breathe here. I tell Francis we shouldn't even bother coming out. It's no different than New York anymore."

"I agree."

"And the way people drive. It's like the Indianapolis 500. I don't even like to get on the roads. It's all tailgating and passing and light flashing. Terrible. Terrible."

Chad stopped massaging. He felt like smacking her, for some reason.

"I never knew what everyone sees in the Hamptons," he said.

"Neither do I. I'd much rather be in France. Now, France I like. You have the food, the wine. And the French people have class and style, not like all the jerks here."

"I've never been there."

"Oh, you should go. Everyone should go to France. You'd never come back if you did."

Penny stopped pedaling and got off the bike. She went over to the bed and laid on her stomach.

"Chad, can you massage me over here?" she said, her face buried in the pillow. "I'm tired of riding the bike."

Chad went over to the bed and continued the massage.

"Have you heard much about the movie?" he said.

"Which one?"

"The one Francis is shooting out here with Jack Hawker."

"Francis never tells me what he's up to. I hardly ever see him. This house is so big, we can both be here and not even know it."

"He'll have to replace Seth Donahue. Maybe you can try to get me an audition."

"Chad, we've been through this before. Francis is very touchy about auditioning friends."

"But I'm not his friend. Can you try?"

Penny flipped onto her back.

"Do my front. I like when you do my front."

Chad started on her stomach. It still felt soft and spongy after three years of his training. Chad hadn't actually expected her to agree to talk to Francis about him. That's okay, Penny, he thought, his ambivalence for her tipping toward dislike. What goes around comes around.

"Does that feel good, Penny?"

"Feels great. Take off my Danskin, please."

Chad did, then found the bottle of baby oil beneath the bed and squirted some on his palm. He rubbed his hands together to warm the oil before laying them on her large, fairly shapely breasts.

"Ummm!" Penny moaned, her eyes closed now.

Chad began to gently knead her breasts and decided to reenact a scene from a movie he'd been in. It would make the task at hand more pleasant for him.

"Who's in control now, Penny?" he said, unable to remember the lines exactly.

"You are, Chad," Penny said.

"That's right. I am," Chad improvised. "I can give you pleasure and I can stop giving you pleasure any time I want."

"Give me pleasure."

"Say please."

"Please."

"Say please give me pleasure."

"Please give me pleasure."

"I already am. Are you saying I'm not? Because if you are, I'm insulted."

"Yes, you are. You always do."

Chad leaned down and spoke into her ear.

"That's right. I always do."

"You're my sexy beast." Penny purred.

"Don't call me a beast."

"I'm sorry."

"Yes, you are."

Chad let his hands glide down her stomach to her vagina. He didn't touch it. He let his fingers hover over it, instead. Penny quivered. Then Chad stood and looked down at her. He began to pace from one side of the bed to the other. Not only did this play into Penny's fantasy, it gave him more time to think and plan. He sat beside her again.

"What have you done to deserve me?" he said.

"Nothing."

"That's right. Nothing." He spread her legs and slipped

his index finger inside of her. "I'm not going to fuck you today, Penny."

"No?" Penny gasped.

"You didn't work hard enough. You didn't even break a sweat."

"I was tired." Penny bit her lower lip. "I drank too much last night."

"That's your fault, not mine."

Chad worked his finger in and out of her. Penny started to moan.

"Do me, Chad."

"I said no."

Penny opened her eyes and Chad could see anger flashing in them now.

"All right, enough playing around, Chad. Do me, okay?"

Chad pulled his finger out of her and wiped it on the bedspread. Again, he wanted to smack her. Don't blow it, he told himself. Don't blow it.

"Hurry up, Chad," Penny snapped. "I have an appointment at the spa in an hour."

"Sorry. I didn't know."

"That's okay. I mean, I like to play a little bit, but sometimes it goes on too long."

"You're definitely right, Penny."

Chad began to undress, and as he did, he conjured the image of the bound woman with his feet propped on her back. He immediately became erect. He spread Penny's legs further and pushed himself into her.

"God, you feel great, Chad," Penny said, in lust again.

Chad began to pump into her, making sure to stop and grind against her every few minutes. He banished the bound-woman fantasy from his mind. He didn't need it anymore. His hard-on wasn't going anywhere at this point. And he wouldn't need the fantasy to help him come. He had no intention of coming. Too much work.

PART THREE

JULY

Riptides have drowned three people by the middle of July: one at Main Beach in East Hampton, one at Sagg Main Beach in Bridgehampton, and one at Cryder Beach in Southampton. The riptides are caused by bottom gullies carved by the winter storms. Like a gun barrel concentrating the discharge of a bullet, these gullies funnel and strengthen the natural undertow. Those caught in it would do best to let it take them out, then swim parallel to the beach until free of its grip. Most swimmers don't know this. Those that do often forget. The three that drowned died flailing futilely for the shore.

The heat has intensified by now. The tomatoes have ripened and the corn would dwarf even the tallest basketball player. The crowds and traffic on the East End have grown, as well, jamming the roads and packing the stores and bars. The locals are making good money off these summer people so far. They always do.

The summer people. More come each year. Those not yet having a good time, assure themselves that they will soon. Many have stopped going into the water for fear of being pulled out and drowned. They bake on the beach instead, eyeing the ocean from time to time. Some try to escape the crowds by reading *Meadow Star*, the hot new novel by Alice Peach, the hot new author. Still others drive themselves crazy wondering if something better and more exciting is happening in a part of the Hamptons they aren't at. These ones are easy to spot, the perpetual look of anxiety etched onto their faces, their quick steps and aggressive manner of driving, often with a cell phone pressed to one ear. It never occurs to them that they might be happier not coming to the Hamptons. The thought doesn't even cross their mind.

CHAPTER

9

Jack pulled off Lily Pond Lane and stopped the Porsche at the head of his driveway. He left the engine running. "Watch this," he said to Andrew.

He got out and walked to the other side of the street, where Karla Sands sat in her BMW, pretending to read a map. When she realized she'd been spotted, she rolled down her window and smiled at Jack. Furball began to growl.

"Hi, Jack."

"Karla Sands parked outside my house on such a beautiful afternoon," Jack said. "What a coincidence."

Karla gestured to Lily Pond Lane.

"I was just admiring your street, Jack. It's wonderful."

"It's no different than any other around here."

Furball's growl deepened. Karla spanked her head.

"Don't growl at Jack Hawker, Furball. You've seen his movies and you thought they were brilliant."

Jack glared at Furball, and the dog put her head down between her paws.

"She gets very protective of me," Karla said. "Don't take it personally."

"I never take dogs personally. What are you doing here,

Karla? If you wanted to invite me to lunch, you should have called."

Karla laughed, nervously.

"That's not a bad idea. Would you like to have lunch with me? My treat."

"Lunch is for assholes, Karla. I bet you eat lunch every day."

Jack turned around as if to walk away. But he undid his belt and pants instead. He lowered them to just below his ass, then pushed it through Karla's window, and farted directly into her car.

"Have that for an appetizer," he said.

He pulled up his pants and walked back to his Porsche.

"You see that, Andrew?" he said, getting in, still buckling his belt.

"Who was that?"

"Karla Sands. The one who tried to pump you for information at Tropper's party."

"And you just stuck your ass in her window, if I'm not mistaken."

"That's right. She said she wanted to have lunch, so I figured I'd give her something to chew on."

Jack laughed and slapped Andrew's knee, then drove to the end of his driveway, which wound snake-like through a perfectly manicured lawn. It made a circle around an island of tulips in front of his gray cedar house, built in the beach bungalow style popular during the Seventies. Jack didn't own it, but he'd paid a hundred and twenty grand to use it during the filming of *A Death in the Hamptons*.

Andrew had never been to the house, so Jack gave him a quick tour. The rooms looked even larger than they were because they contained almost no furniture. The living room had been built on three levels and it flowed into an open kitchen. The late afternoon light streamed through the huge windows. A sliding door led out onto a wooden deck that featured a jacuzzi, a bar and a panoramic view of the

Atlantic. Jack went behind the bar and poured himself a Jamesons. He opened a Heineken for Andrew.

"Sorry, no Budweiser," he said.

"I'll make do."

They sat on lounge chairs and Jack shook his head at what had just happened with Karla outside.

"You see, there're two types in my business," he said. "Either you're the talent or you not. And if you're not, you're a leech that feeds off the talent. That Karla Sands is the worst kind of leech. The lowest of the low."

"Why are you even in this business, if it's so bad?"

"Power. That's why," Jack said, without hesitation. "Look at our society. Who're the most powerful people in it? It's not the politicians, I'll tell you that. It's not the doctors and scientists, either. It's not the cops or even guys like you who provide the food. It's bullshit Hollywood actors like me. We're the ones who capture people's imaginations. We're the ones with the power to take them out of their little worlds, give them something to dream about and lust after. And we have money. That doesn't hurt."

"I'm sure it doesn't," Andrew said, looking out at a fishing trawler far off shore. He took a mouthful of Heineken and decided he liked it better than Budweiser.

Jack gazed down to the beach, at a young woman in a string bikini.

"Tail everywhere you look," he said softly. "I could rule the world if I didn't waste all my energy chasing tail."

Andrew looked at the woman, too, and experienced a wave of lust.

"Doesn't seem like you need to put much energy into it," he said.

"You should speak for yourself. Old Gwendolyn isn't as easy to bed as you might think."

Andrew's encounter with her on the beach had happened more than a month ago. He hadn't seen her since.

"You still don't mind about that?" he said.

"I'm a true friend. I like to share."

Andrew finished his beer and started to feel sleepy. He couldn't help yawning.

"Bored already?" Jack said.

"No. Tired."

"Take a nap in the guest room. I don't want to wear you out."

Jack's guest room had a king-sized bed and a black teak armoire in it.

Andrew lowered the Venetian blinds and the room became nighttime dark. He undressed and climbed under the sheet, but couldn't sleep right away. He lay there looking up at the slanted ceiling, listening to the ocean. It sounded like someone breathing. The room felt hot, but he didn't have the energy to get up and open the window. He heard Jack talking on a cordless phone outside his door. "Excellent. Excellent," Jack said. "I wouldn't trust anyone but you with it."

Jack moved away from the door and his voice faded until Andrew couldn't hear it anymore. He started thinking about little Charlie and Annie and suddenly became very sad. Not because of anything specific that had happened, but because he felt so distant from them now, as if they existed in a different world, across a divide he would never be able to cross. It occurred to him that his life had been pretty good until it went bad, until the morning he woke up and didn't know his wife anymore, until he realized he didn't know himself very well, either.

He considered getting out of bed and leaving. He knew he had no business spending time with a guy like Jack Hawker, a man with no moral compass that he could detect. And he sensed that Jack wanted more from him than just research. He had expressed almost no interest in him as a fisherman so far. Nuances? Mannerisms? As far as Andrew could tell, he possessed none anyone should be interesting in learning.

He began to drift off. And in the purgatory between sleep and wakefulness, he sensed someone in the room with him. He sat up and looked around, but saw no one there. He lay back down and fell asleep this time. But he slept shallowly and immediately went into a dream, one hard to distinguish from reality.

The dream had him driving Jack's Porsche along a winding back road that he'd been on before. But he couldn't recall the name of it, and he became lost as it took him deeper and deeper into the woods. He drove for what seemed like a long time, losing all his bearings. He saw someone standing in the road ahead and decided to stop and ask him for directions. But as he approached, the man didn't move from the middle of the road. He just stood there, and as Andrew came closer, he saw that it was Seth Donahue. Seth's skin looked as white as parchment paper, and he wore the same wraparound sunglasses Sugar B had at Tropper's party. Andrew stopped the car and Seth remained in the middle of the road, as still as a statue, staring at him through the windshield. Andrew noticed the wound across his neck, a deep gash crudely stitched together. Then Seth took off his sunglasses and Andrew could see that he had no eyes, just black holes where they had once been. Seth smiled and took a step toward the car. Andrew threw it into reverse and hit the gas, but the wheels spun, refusing to grip. He got out and began to run, into the woods, as fast as he could, weaving through the thicket of vines and prickers. Soon he came to a halt in a clearing where Charlie and Annie were playing together. His children didn't notice him at first, then looked up and beckoned him forward. A wave of relief washed over Andrew. It's okay, he thought. Just a dream. I'm awake now. He approached his children and could hear them talking to each other. He crouched beside Annie and she turned and held a Barbie doll out to him. Andrew noticed its head had been ripped off. When he looked at Annie again, her face had became Gwendolyn's.

"I did this, daddy," she said, in Gwendolyn's tired voice. "I killed her."

Andrew woke and found Jack standing beside the bed in the dark, looking down at him. The sheets were soaked with sweat.

"What, did you piss the bed?" Jack said.

"I was having another nightmare."

"You seem to have a lot of them."

"Yeah, lately."

"Get dressed. We'll take a drive."

Jack left the room and Andrew got out of bed. He waited for his sweat to dry before putting on his clothes.

CHAPTER

10

"Driving calms me," Jack said.

He wasn't driving calmly, though. He'd decided to take East Hampton's back roads: Further Lane to Dunemere to James to Georgica, which led to the Highway, which he took as far as Southampton. He drove past mansions and estates, some hidden behind tall, sculpted hedgerows, most set back from the road at the end of long, freshly paved driveways. Andrew had never driven those roads himself. His daily route took him from his house to the dock, then to Moran's in the evenings. He seldom ventured west from Montauk to the Hamptons.

The Southampton sidewalks were crowded with shoppers and browsers when they got there. Jack joined the traffic along Main Street and watched the women as he moved slowly forward. Andrew watched them, too, wondering if they would look so good without the money to pay for their hair and clothes, makeup and surgery. Jack looped back around to the highway at the end of Main Street, then turned onto Sandy Hollow Road, which became North Sea Road in a couple of miles.

He followed North Sea Road through the woods, and he

seemed unusually preoccupied as he drove. Andrew didn't feel like forcing conversation, so he looked out the window as they passed the old German deli, then Rocket nightclub. He'd heard that lots of celebrities went there. Then he started wondering what exactly he was doing with Jack Hawker, where it might lead him. He couldn't come to any conclusion, other than that the "Friendship" arrangement they'd made, whatever that meant, was making him uneasy.

The road forked and Jack bore right onto Noyac Road, driving fast despite the sharpening curves and steepening hills. Noyac Road took them north across the fork, then flattened along the Peconic as it turned east, transversing its inlets and small back bays on the way to Sag Harbor. The late afternoon sun had spread over these flat, protected waters, the headlands molding each into a distinct size and shape. Sea grass sprouted from their shallows and a couple of kayakers paddled through a thick stand of bulrushes. A long stretch of shore called Long Beach formed a gently curving horseshoe just before Sag Harbor. People swam and sunbathed along it, and men fished off the rocks at its eastern end. Andrew tried to see if they were catching anything.

Jack turned right after Long Beach, onto South Ferry Road and over the bridge that led into Sag Harbor. He drove up the winding main street, past the American Hotel, its elegant porch filled with drinkers. He bore left at the top of the street and headed toward East Hampton on Route 114. He turned onto Long Lane before arriving in East Hampton, and it took them past a duck farm and through a corn field with puffy, white clouds hanging over it. It looked like a painting, the waning light possessing an etheral quality that Andrew often admired from behind *Bessie*'s wheel.

"Aren't many farms left out here," Jack said.

"It's too bad."

"It's progress. You can't stop it."

They hit the straight, flat Napeague stretch after passing through East Hampton and Amagansett. Beach houses and condominiums nestled amongst the dunes on either side, and

Lobster Roll was crowded with tourists, as always. Andrew knew the owner. He'd made a fortune over the years. Jack bore right at the end of Napeague, and took the Old Montauk Highway instead of the new one. The road resembled a rollercoaster as it ran along the dunes, past Hither Hills State Park and Gurney's Spa and the E.B. White mailbox that belonged to someone with the same name as the late writer. Jack didn't hit the brakes once and Andrew held tightly to his door handle, each swoop registering in the pit of his stomach, reminding him of *Bessie* on a rough day.

"We'll go out to the Point," Jack said, as they crested a rise and Montauk came into view.

Montauk has a different look and feel than the Hamptons. The beach and the ocean have a stronger presence, drifted sand and beach motels lining the road leading into town. Most of the motels were built years ago and the constant salt wind has given them a pleasantly worn appearance. Jack accelerated up the hill on the east side of town and drove the six miles to the Point in less than fifteen minutes. He parked in the lot there and they walked a path through the thicket down to the rocky beach at the base of the lighthouse. The water was rough here at the end of the island. It hit the outer rocks hard and sent spray far enough to wet the concrete reinforcing wall beneath the red and white striped lighthouse.

Andrew followed Jack out onto a jetty where fishermen stood with surfcasters. Jack asked one if he'd caught anything, and the fisher pointed at a large blue laid out on a rock, its gills struggling to filter oxygen from the air. Jack stopped and poked the fish with his finger, then moved on to the end of the jetty where the waves broke, sending up a fine spray. He sat on a damp rock and Andrew sat beside him. He opened his mouth and tasted the familiar sea salt. He looked back at the bluefish dying on the rock, and then turned to Jack.

"So, tell me what you want from me, Jack."

Jack snapped out of his ocean stare.

"What do you mean?"

"I mean, what are we doing together?"

"We're sitting on a jetty. What do you think?"

"What I think is you don't need me. You haven't asked me one thing about fishing."

Jack seemed to be searching his brain for a fishing question he could ask Andrew. But all he said was, "You're my man, Andrew. I need you for this film."

"I'm sure you can do it without me."

Jack put his hand on Andrew's shoulder.

"Andrew. Andy boy. What's the matter? You're not having fun?"

"I didn't say that."

"Haven't I taken you to a nice party? Didn't I get you laid—with a movie star, no less?"

"That's true, but—"

"If I hadn't shown up at Moran's that night, you'd be sitting there right now, pining after that barmaid."

Andrew thought of Katie. He *would* be at Moran's right now, undoubtedly sneaking glances across the bar at her.

"It's not that," he said. "I just don't know what the purpose of this is."

"There doesn't always have to be a purpose to everything."

Andrew couldn't argue with that.

"I have to make a living, you know," he said. "I can't just go running around like you do."

"I'll pay you what you need."

"I don't want your money."

Jack took a hundred dollar bill from his wallet and slipped it into Andrew's shirt pocket.

"Don't be so fucking proud," he said.

Andrew let the money stay in his pocket, but it only made him feel worse. He returned it to Jack and stood.

"I appreciate the offer, but I have to get going."

He began to walk the jetty toward the beach, but turned around before he got there. He looked at Jack sitting by himself and suddenly felt sorry for him, just another lonely guy now, not a big movie star. He returned to Jack and could see moisture had gathered in the corners of his eyes.

"Sorry, Jack. I didn't mean to be so harsh."

Jack didn't respond at first. He rubbed away his tears.

"Don't be sorry," he said. "I'm just feeling a little lonely, lately."

"You? Lonely?"

"Who would have thought, right? Sometimes I forget that I am, but sitting here looking at the ocean reminds me. The truth is I don't have many friends, Andrew, not real ones."

"That's too bad."

Jack sniffled and wiped his nose with his arm. He managed to smile.

"The world's a funny place," he said. "But enough heavy stuff for one day. Let's go get a drink."

They went to the Red Monkey in East Hampton, decorated in a tropical, Jimmy Buffet/Key West motif. The bar had already filled with drinkers who'd spent most of the day on the beach. They found two stools and Jack ordered margaritas. The bartender, wearing a Hawaiian print shirt, brought bowls of chips and salsa along with the drinks. Andrew began eating them, but the margarita got to his stomach first.

A woman with sandy-colored hair came over and asked Jack for an autograph.

"Only if you give me a kiss," Jack told her. The woman did and Jack kept his end of the bargain, scrawling his name on a cocktail napkin. The woman returned to her table, where a bunch of her girlfriends sat eyeing Jack.

"It must be nice having any woman you want," Andrew said.

"You just have to exude the right energy, my man."

"Being a movie star doesn't hurt."

"You should try it some day."

Andrew tried to imagine what being a movie star would be like. He finished his margarita quickly. The tequila in it was having a more altering effect on him than beer did. Jack ordered another round.

"Here's to friendship," he said, before drinking.

"Nothing more important."

This margarita tasted even better than the first. And as Andrew drank it, he allowed himself to bask in Jack's glow. More women approached. Jack introduced one to Andrew, a petite young girl with large, brown eyes.

"I'm working on Jack's film," Andrew told her. "It's called *A Death in the Hamptons.*"

"What's it about?"

"An East End fisherman, like me."

Andrew was starting to feel a bit drunk, a happy drunk, though, full of hope and expectation.

"What are you doing on the movie?" the girl asked him.

"I'm a consultant."

"Do you like being a film consultant?"

"It's a living, like anything else."

The time passed quickly and Andrew lost count of how many margaritas he drank. He kept talking to the girl, who soon became the prettiest girl he'd ever seen. He considered proposing to her right there in the Red Monkey. The bar-room beyond his line of sight became blurred, and next to him, Jack had spun his stool to face the women now crowd-ed around him.

"I'm in love with all of you," Jack said. "Every single one."

The women laughed, an undercurrent of longing and competition in their laughter. Andrew found himself kissing the petite girl he'd been talking to. He couldn't remember how they started doing it, but her lips felt so soft and good, her long, straight hair feathering against his cheek. She moved between his legs and worked her tongue against his. Andrew didn't care who watched. He didn't know anyone in the bar, and only vaguely recognized the bartender. Through the haze of sounds, he heard a man say, "You're a phony, Hawker. You know that?"

The man's harsh tone jolted Andrew back to reality. He stopped kissing the girl and saw a large man with a shaved head standing in front of Jack. He noticed the man's jaws working, as if chewing a piece of gristle. Jack's women had moved aside.

"What makes you say that?" Jack said to the man. "I'm just here having some drinks and a few laughs."

The man's fists were clenched. He was clearly drunk.

"You come in here and act like you own the place," he said. "Has anyone ever told you your movies suck?"

"Only the critics, my friend. Only the critics."

Andrew suddenly felt quite sober. The girl he'd been kissing had stepped away from him.

"Did you happen to see *Fire Fight II?*" Jack said to the man.

"Yeah, I saw it."

"Then you probably remember this scene."

Without any more warning, Jack unleashed a hard kick to the man's balls. The man doubled over and Jack calmly grabbed his ears and pulled his face forward. Andrew heard a pop as the man's nose broke against Jack's knee. He saw the spurt of blood. The bar had quieted, and U2's "In the Name of Love" playing on the jukebox suddenly sounded surreally loud. Everyone in the place had turned to watch Jack's demonstration, including the bartender, who didn't seem to know what else to do. Jack placed his hand on the man's forehead and pushed him upright.

"I'm sure you remember the scene now," he said. "It's the one where I kick the guy's ass without even leaving my barstool."

The man remained on his feet until Jack knocked him to the ground with a straight right to his face. Jack then got off his stool and delivered a double kick to his foe's ribcage, using his left foot first, then his right. The fallen man let out a grunt as each blow landed.

"How'd you like the double kick?" Jack said to Andrew. "It wasn't in the movie. I just made it up."

He administered another one, then sat again and ordered a fresh round of margaritas. His women had returned to their table and Andrew's petite girl had disappeared alto-gether. A couple of patrons helped the fallen man to his feet and out of the bar. Andrew couldn't believe what he had just seen. He'd witnessed bar fights before, but nothing as brutal as this.

"Self-defense, Andrew," Jack said, noticing the look on Andrew's face.

"Was it?"

"Sure. Why not?"

The bartender brought the drinks.

"You know any jokes?" Jack asked him.

The bartender shook his head, too scared to look Jack in the eye.

"What kind of bartender doesn't know any jokes?" Jack said. He drank some of his new margarita and turned to Andrew. "I know of a party we can go to later."

CHAPTER 11

They scheduled their session later than usual because Penny wanted to continue her nap. She'd been to the East Hampton Beach Club earlier that day and the social interaction there had exhausted her. She never set foot on the beach when she went to the club, too ashamed of her figure. She'd stay up on the deck instead, drinking iced tea and chit-chatting with the other members about nothing important or interesting. She didn't enjoy the club, but felt obligated to put in an appearance every once in a while. She knew she risked being ostracized if she didn't, or forgotten.

Chad knocked on her bedroom door and heard Penny murmur, "Come in."

He went in and found the room dark except for a night-light in the bathroom. He put his gym bag down and went over to the bed, where Penny lay curled beneath a silk sheet. She had on a bra and panties, nothing else. Chad sat on the bed beside her.

"I'm sooo tired, Chad. I can't wake up."

"It's time to work out. We're late already."

Penny pulled the sheet over her head.

"I can't," she said. "I'm too tired."

"What do you want to do, then?"

"I just want to lie here. Rest is good for you too, isn't it?"

"But if you don't work out, you'll never want to go on the beach. Didn't you tell me that was your goal this summer, to get in good enough shape to go on the beach?"

Penny rolled away from him.

"Oh, what's the point?"

Chad eyed the wandering jew. It still seemed like his best bet.

"Feeling good about yourself is the point," he said.

"Spoon me, Chad."

Chad almost told her no, but then did as he'd been told. He lay down beside her, turned, and molded his body against hers. Penny reached back and pulled his arms around her.

"Just for a few minutes," Chad said.

"Don't worry. I'm paying you for the session."

"I'm not worried about that."

They lay there for a while. Then Penny said, "My mother and I used to do this when I was a little girl."

"Where did you grow up?" Chad didn't particularly care to know.

"Brooklyn," Penny said. "Flatbush. Ever hear of it?"

"I think so. Did you have a good childhood?" Chad felt somewhat obligated to keep her entertained. She *was* paying him, after all.

"I had a lousy childhood. It really wasn't much of a childhood." Penny wriggled her butt into his groin. "I remember when I was a girl I wanted to be Miss America. I'd spend hours in front of the mirror making myself look beautiful. And you know what? It worked. I was beautiful once, years ago."

It was true. Chad had seen pictures of Penny as a young woman. They were all over the house. She resembled a young Liz Taylor.

"I've seen pictures of you," Chad said. "You were very beautiful."

"I was," Penny said.

"You still are."

"I'm forty-one, Chad. I'm not beautiful anymore."

Chad rubbed her stomach some.

"How come you didn't have much of a childhood?" he said.

"My father left when I was two. He took up with another woman in California. A little girl can't have a childhood without a father."

"What about your mother?"

"Oh, she drank a lot. She didn't pay much attention to me. Could you rub my shoulders?"

Chad began to massage her shoulders. It was awkward and tiring to do it from this position, but he did it as best he could. Keep her happy, he thought. Just keep her happy. Penny turned over to face him.

"No more massage?" Chad said.

Penny had wistful expression on her face now. It made him uneasy.

"You're attractive, Chad, in an off-beat kind of way."

"What do you mean, off-beat?"

"There was a time when I could have any attractive man I wanted."

No sob stories, please, Chad thought, wishing he could escape now. But since he couldn't, he let his thoughts take him away. He thought about the trip to the city he would be making in a day or two. He already knew exactly which store he would visit to buy what he needed. No wasting time shopping around.

"You could still get any man you wanted," he said.

"That's kind of you, Chad. Now lay on your back so I can put my head on your chest."

Chad did and Penny nestled her head on his chest. He began to stroke her hair. Women are like little girls, he thought. They like having their hair stroked. Penny closed her eyes and Chad suspected she was imagining he was someone else, her long lost father, perhaps, or maybe the man she should have married. He kept stroking her hair and hoped she would fall asleep. He looked at the digital clock on the night table. Forty minutes remained in their session. He stared up at the ceiling and tried to think of scenes for his screenplay, but drew a blank. It's going to be good, though. Damn good. Then Penny said, "Francis is gay, you know. He wasn't when I married him. At least, I don't think he was."

"Why don't you divorce him?"

"It's not so easy."

Chad suspected she was referring to the money, not the kids or the marriage itself. It wouldn't be easy giving up such a lavish lifestyle, which was what she would have to do if she divorced him. Because Francis would certainly hire the best lawyer in New York. Penny wouldn't stand a chance.

"What about your kids?" he said.

"Yeah, the kids. I'm sure it all looks so good from the outside. If people only knew. It's humiliating."

"Well, your secret's safe with me."

"I'm glad I can trust you."

"You can always trust me."

Penny nestled deeper into Chad's chest and let her arm fall across his stomach. She may as well be talking to a dog, Chad thought. She wouldn't have told all that to someone she thought of as being on her level.

"We're going to a dinner party at the Channings tonight," Penny said.

"Who are the Channings?"

"He's some kind of big shot banker. I don't want to go. I never know what to say to those people."

"Just be yourself."

"I try to. It doesn't always work. Maybe I should become an alcoholic like my mother. At least she had that."

Chad laughed.

"Don't be silly."

"Maybe I'll just stay here in bed. I'll pretend I'm sick."

"That would only make you feel worse."

"I know."

Chad checked the clock. He couldn't wait for this to be over. He preferred having sex with her to this.

"We only have twenty-five more minutes, Penny."

"Spank me, Chad. I think I need a good spanking."

"Why?"

"Because I . . . I don't know. I just want one. Hard enough to hurt me but not hard enough to really hurt."

Penny lifted her head off Chad's chest and flipped onto her stomach. Chad pulled the sheet away and half-heartedly smacked her ass.

"On my bare ass," Penny said, into the pillow.

Chad pulled down her panties and looked at her butt. He could tell it had once been fairly well formed. He knew he could work it back into shape if Penny wasn't so damned lazy. He smacked it again. His hand left an imprint.

"Harder," Penny said, squirming a bit.

Chad spanked her harder and continued doing it for ten straight minutes. Penny let out a little yelp with each smack and her ass was soon red all over. Afterward, she lay there breathing hard, as if she had been transported by the pain.

"Was that good, Penny?"

"Very."

Penny fell asleep a few minutes later, and Chad got out of the bed. He opened his gym bag and took from it the video camera he'd bought. He tiptoed over to the hanging plant and gently placed the camera in it, aiming the lens at the bed. He moved some of the leaves so it wouldn't be obstructed. Stepping back, he could tell that, even in the light, no one would see it unless they looked closely. Briefly, he worried that someone might water the plant, but figured it was a risk worth taking. Besides, that kind of plant probably doesn't need much watering. This is going to work, he thought, slinging his gym bag over his shoulder. On his way out of the room, he spotted last month's issue of *Boulevard Magazine* on the floor. He picked it up and took it with him. He had nothing else to read.

CHAPTER 12

Once again, Ralph and Donny were there at Moran's. Once again, Andrew wasn't. Katie looked over at his empty stool, then returned to what she had been thinking about. She could no longer ignore the fact that she was getting older, with no husband or kids to show for it. It's this place, she thought, shaking excess water from the pint glass she'd just washed. To hell with the legacy. I have to get out here.

Donny lit a cigarette.

"Gee, where's Andrew tonight?" he said, making no effort to conceal his sarcasm.

Ralph shook his head.

"Ever since he found that body, he hasn't been the same."

"Ever since he met that Jack Hawker, he hasn't been the same."

"How would you guys know?" Katie said. "He's barely been in since then."

Neither Donny nor Ralph could deny it. Satisfied that she'd hushed those two, Katie finished cleaning glasses, then busied herself turning the labels of the top shelf bottles forward.

"I've been worried about him," Ralph said. "Maybe he's still out of sorts about his divorce."

Donny blew a smoke ring.

"You think he'll ever find another woman?"

"In Montauk? I doubt it."

Katie stopped facing the bottles, momentarily thrown by the idea of Andrew finding another woman some day. She recalled that morning on the beach after the prom, how badly she'd wanted to kiss him then. Even so many years later, it felt strange to contemplate it. She looked behind her and found his stool still empty. She finished facing the bottles, then picked up the *New York Times* and began reading an article about a corrupt accounting firm.

"Why are you always reading the *Times*, Katie?" Ralph said.

"You should try reading it yourself someday. It might clear the cobwebs out of your brain."

"Me read the *New York Times*? C'mon, I'm not Jewish."

Katie knew better than to even try to interpret that one. Like many of the local fishermen, Ralph had a good heart but could hardly be called enlightened.

"You guys want another round?"

"Does a fish shit in water?" Donny said.

Katie got them two bottles of Budweiser. She never had to ask what they wanted. She went back to her perch beside the register and tried to read again, but couldn't help thinking about Andrew instead, wondering where he was, what he was doing.

"I bet he's with Jack Hawker right now," Donny said, as if reading Katie's thoughts.

"You think so?" Ralph said.

"I've heard they've been spotted palling around. Real buddyroos."

"Celebrities like Jack Hawker don't impress me."

"He doesn't impress me either," Donny snapped. "Did I say he impresses me?"

"I didn't say you said that."

"Good. Because I didn't and he doesn't."

"Me neither."

"All right, then."

They each tilted some beer into their mouths. Then Donny slammed down his bottle and grabbed both sides of his head, as if to keep it from splitting open.

"Well, fuck me dry!" he shouted. "It's the movie!"

"The movie?" Ralph said.

"The fisherman one Jack Hawker's going to make here this summer. I bet that sonofabitch Andrew already has a part in it."

"How do you figure?"

"Don't be stupid, Ralph. It's a movie about fishermen. That night Hawker came here, he was recruiting. It's obvious."

"And just our luck, me and you leave before he comes in."

Donny drank more beer.

"That's why Andrew doesn't show anymore," he said. "He's going to be a big fuckin' movie star. He probably figures he doesn't need friends like us anymore."

"You're insane, Donny," Katie said. "You know that?"

She went to the end of the bar and looked out at the bay and the dark outline of Gardiners Island. Donny let out a snort behind her.

"Some guys live charmed fucking lives," he said, bitterness edging his voice. "He catches an actor's body that morning, and that night he goes out with Jack Hawker and gets a part in a movie. Go figure."

Katie came back from the window.

"Yeah, real charmed," she said. "He pulls a headless body from the water and he'll probably have nightmares for the rest of his life."

"At least it's exciting," Donny grumbled. "Man, what I'd do for some excitement." He turned to Ralph. "Play some pool?"

"Dollar a game?"

"Nah. Let's just play."

They went to the table and Ralph racked the balls. But neither of them shot with much conviction. Katie picked up an *East Hampton Star* someone had left behind. She started to skim a front page article about the ongoing Seth Donahue investigation just as the door opened. Katie half-expected it to be Andrew. Sheriff Pete Moran walked in instead, looking tired and beat. Pete waved to Donny and Ralph, and took a stool at the bar.

"Hey, Uncle Pete. Get you a beer?"

Pete took off his hat and put it on the bar in front of him.

"No, thanks, sweety. I'm still working. I thought I might find Andrew here."

"He hasn't been in in weeks."

"Finding that body did a number on him, huh?"

"I guess. Who knows? Andrew never volunteers anything."

"Yeah, well, I was hoping he could volunteer some more information about what happened."

Katie frowned.

"He's not a suspect, is he?"

"No, no. I just wonder if he can remember something that might help me. So far forensics says it was done with an army machete." Pete threw up his hands. "Any veteran might have one. Hell, you can buy a machete at most Army/Navy stores."

Katie drew a glass of water for her uncle.

"But what else could Andrew tell you?" she said. "All he did was find the body."

Pete drank most of the water and ran his finger through his thick gray hair.

"I don't know, Katie. Maybe he can tell me which way the currents were moving that morning. That could help determine where the body came from. It might lead me to something. I'm grasping at straws now, to tell you the truth."

"You sure you don't want a beer, uncle Pete?"

Pete waved away the offer.

"Water's fine. I need every brain cell working for this one." He rubbed his temples and let out a sigh. "I was hoping to retire in a few months without any unfinished business hanging over me."

Katie refilled his glass.

"You're doing what you can. That's all you can do."

"I know. But this town's been my responsibility for nearly thirty years and I don't want to leave this unsolved." Pete looked around the bar, as if seeing it for the first time. "I remember when Montauk was a quieter place. Now it's like the world is trying to push us off the island."

He stood and put on his hat.

"You might try his house," Katie said.

"I already did. Not home. If you see him, tell him to give me a call."

"Get some rest, Uncle Pete."

"I'll try. This case is making it hard, though."

Katie watched her uncle leave, then went back to the window. A cloud had covered the moon, making it more difficult to see the water and Gardiner's Island now. She stayed at the window for a while, feeling especially trapped tonight, hoping the rest of it would pass quickly.

CHAPTER

13

Although built only a few years ago, the mansion in Southampton was designed to look like an old English manor house: brown shingles, a slate roof and a lawn jockey out front, its face and hands painted white. Cars filled the long, bluestone driveway. More were parked along Wyandanch Lane for blocks in either direction. The lights inside the house were barroom dim and loud music pounded from giant floor speakers; no lyrics or melody, just a driving beat.

The Red Monkey margaritas still had a hold on Andrew. Nothing besides chips and salsa stood in their way. Jack had talked about the fight the entire way from the Red Monkey, describing the different moves and tactics he would use in his next one.

"You think that guy's going to be okay?" Andrew said.

"Who cares? He started it."

They entered the house and the crowd inside looked younger and looser than the one at Tropper's party. Andrew didn't recognize anyone there except for Allen Balford.

Balford was speaking to a woman in stiletto heels and a clingy wrap dress, alternating sips between the two drinks he held in either hand. Balford's eyes kept dropping to the woman's cleavage as he spoke to her. He glanced over her shoulder at Jack and Andrew when they walked in, then looked back at her breasts without skipping a word or missing a beat.

Jack and Andrew headed toward the bar. On the way there, they encountered an elegant-looking middle-aged man with dark, thinning hair. He seemed over-dressed in his tan Armani suit. He held his martini glass by its stem and he was observing the party with a bemused smile on his pinched, hawkish face.

"Andrew, this is Lander Sobel," Jack said. "You need a Picasso or a Pollack, you come to Lander."

Lander shook Andrew's hand. His fingers felt thin, his grip delicate.

"Pleased to meet you, Andrew," Lander said, with a slight English accent. "Jack's told me you'll be working on the film with him."

"Well, not really."

"I happen to think it's going to be excellent," Lander said.

"Me, too."

"Oh? Have you read the script?"

"Just a few lines."

"Then how can you have an opinion?"

Andrew saw no humor anywhere on Lander's face. He heard none in his voice.

"What I meant is I think Jack will play a good fisherman."

"And I assume you think that's because of your input."

"No, I think that's because he's a good actor."

Lander's eyes widened and he raised his brows.

"Oh, you're a critic," he said.

"Not exactly."

"Then you shouldn't make pronouncements about things you know very little about."

Andrew gave himself a moment to collect his thoughts.

He considered walking away, but didn't want to humiliate himself in front of Jack.

"Did I say something to offend you, Mr. Sobel?"

"You haven't said anything with enough weight to offend anyone."

"I just gave my opinion, that's all."

"Some opinions are better left unexpressed. If I wanted to know about fishing, perhaps I would ask you. Films? No."

Andrew looked at Jack, but got no help from him, only a smirk.

"Listen, maybe you and me got off on the wrong foot," he said to Lander.

"We never had a footing to begin with. And it's 'you and I' not 'you and me'."

Jack's smirk gave way to a laugh.

"All right, Lander," he said. "That's enough. You got him pretty good."

Lander smiled and took a sip of his martini.

"I did, didn't I?" He turned back to Andrew. "It's just a little game of mine. A joke. I razz people until they either cry or commit suicide. I did have you there, didn't I?"

"Yeah, you did."

Jack punched Lander's shoulder, lightly. Somehow Lander managed to keep his martini from spilling.

"I think old Lander here likes you, Andrew," Jack said. "He would have torn into you much worse if he didn't."

"I guess I'm lucky," Andrew said. "I think I need a drink."

He went to the bar and ordered a tequila on the rocks. Jack was gone by the time he returned with it. Lander was still there, though. He raised his glass to Andrew. Andrew raised his back, but kept moving until he found an empty spot. He stopped there and drank some tequila and felt the music vibrating through the soles of his shoes. He closed his eyes and swayed with it, then began to move his feet a little. His blood felt hot, literally, and he felt even drunker now than he did in the Red Monkey. He began to sweat, so he undid a shirt button and drank more tequila. He found a woman dancing with him when he opened his eyes, pretty and dark and voluptuous. Her dress fit like a leotard, plunging down her chest, covering her crotch with only inches to spare. She smiled at Andrew, who reached out and touched her throat, letting his finger slide down to the beginning of her cleavage. He drank some more and closed his eyes again. The woman was gone when he opened them, replaced by Allen Balford and his smile. His teeth looked even whiter and straighter than Simone Tropper's.

"You're Jack's friend, aren't you?" Balford said.

"Yeah, I am."

"Having a good time?"

"So far."

Balford gestured to the party.

"This is what the Hamptons are all about."

"That's what I hear."

Balford leaned close to Andrew, as if to tell an important secret.

"It's all about getting laid," he said, pointing to Andrew's crotch. "The rest is just horseshit."

"You're probably right."

"I know I am. It's like peaches. It's all there for the picking if you have what it takes." Balford straightened up, surprised by his own eloquence. "Hey, that's a good one," he said. "I like it. By the way, have you seen Jack?"

"I saw him a minute ago."

"When you see him again, tell him Allen Balford said hello. I'll catch you later."

Balford headed off to the bar and Andrew decided to explore a bit. It seemed the thing to do at parties filled with strangers. He moved across the main room, which was not quite as cavernous as Tropper's. A mirrored disco ball hung from a thin chain and it threw colored light beams in every direction. This and the tequila combined to skew Andrew's balance. He kept bumping into people, but no one seemed

to mind. Someone had turned up the music and more people were dancing now. Andrew spotted Sugar B and his two
henchmen standing in the middle of the dancers, wearing
their sunglasses, their purple suits and their half angry, half
sullen expressions. A toothpick protruded from the corner of
Sugar B's mouth and two women were dancing in front of him.

Andrew kept moving. He watched a couple grope each
other for a few moments, but his eyes and attention couldn't
focus on any particular person or thing for long. The music
seemed to be inside his skull now, pounding, trying to get
out. He couldn't feel his feet touching the floor, either. He
imagined himself floating on a layer of air, like in a dream.
It's the tequila he told himself. Too much tequila. He took
another sip anyway, and could no longer taste it. He felt
someone pinch his ass. He turned and found Gwendolyn
standing there. She seemed like an old friend amidst the
crowd of mostly unfamiliar faces.

"You have a pinchable ass," Gwendolyn said, hooking her
arm in his. "Come with me."

She led him through the crowd and up a staircase.

"Where's Jack?" Andrew said, when they reached the top.

"You two are becoming good friends, aren't you?"

"Sure. Why not?"

Gwendolyn led him down a hallway, to a door at the end.
She opened it and guided Andrew into a small room, then
closed the door behind them. Only candles lit the room, long
white ones planted on every surface, their melting wax dripping into puddles. The flickering flames bounced shadows off
the ceiling and walls. Andrew's eyes soon adjusted and he
could make out figures sitting on long, low couches.

"Andrew has arrived," one of the figures said. It was Jack.

Andrew squinted until he could see his face. It looked different with the candlelight playing over it. He heard someone laugh and could make out Francis Baskin on another
couch, with the captain of *Diablo* perched on his lap. Francis
had his hand buried between the captain's legs and they were

kissing each other on the mouth. Gwendolyn sat beside Jack.

"I think I drank too much," Andrew said.

Jack pulled a pill from his pocket and handed it to him.

"Take this," he said. "It will smooth you out."

Andrew put the pill on his tongue and washed it down with tequila. It had no effect at first. He sat next to Jack and Gwendolyn and felt like he'd passed some undefinable point of no return.

"Nice to see you again, Andrew," Francis drawled from the couch on the other side of the room.

"Nice to see you, too, Francis."

"Andrew, this is Captain Carlos."

Carlos nodded and smiled and resumed kissing Francis. Andrew looked away from them and began to feel woozy. He sat back and Jack put his arm across his shoulder, a rocks glass of whiskey in his hand.

"Ain't this the shit?" Jack said.

"Yeah, the shit," Andrew answered.

From across the room, Carlos said, "No. No." and Francis said, "Yes. Yes."

Andrew drank more tequila without realizing it. He could feel the pill taking effect, making his muscles go slack. He wondered whose party this was and vaguely remembered driving to it with Jack, turning off the highway onto Flying Point Road, then Wyandanch Lane.

"Why are we all up here?" he asked no one in particular. His voice sounded muffled and it seemed to be coming from a distance.

"I can't hang with the amateurs downstairs," Jack said. "How you feeling now?"

"Relaxed. Very relaxed."

Jack nodded.

"No point being uptight."

Andrew noticed someone sitting on the floor against the wall. The candlelight didn't reach that far and he couldn't tell if it was a man or a woman.

"Who's that?" he said, pointing at the person.

"Who do you want it to be?" Jack said.

Andrew began to laugh, unsure exactly why.

The person sitting on the floor got to her feet and stepped out of the shadow. She was tall and young and she looked like a fashion model. She sat on the couch next to Andrew.

"Do you like fishermen?" Andrew said to her.

The woman leaned up against him.

"I think fishermen are very brave," she cooed.

Jack jiggled the ice in his whiskey.

"Courage," he said. "That's what it's really all about."

"Yeah," Andrew said. "Courage."

"You know how many people have it?"

"How many?"

"Very few," Jack said.

"I think you're right."

"I know I'm right. Most see opportunities but are too scared to take them. It all comes back to the death urge I told you about. People would rather go through life half dead. Don't you agree?"

"Makes sense," Andrew said. "Perfect sense."

The woman began to caress his stomach and he closed his eyes to heighten the experience. He heard Francis laughing, then a slap, then no more laughter, just soft moaning.

"The world's going to end one day," Jack said. "When it does, none of this will matter anymore. Everything man has accomplished will be for naught. All the skyscrapers will be flattened, the dams broken, the roads destroyed. Every book will be vaporized, and the knowledge in them will be gone forever. Forests will turn to ash and mountains will be reduced to piles of cinder. What else is there? Oh, yeah. Love. It won't save anything. It's just a word."

Andrew didn't realize his eyes were still shut because Jack's words were painting such vivid pictures in his mind. His voice had taken on a hypnotic quality, a flat mesmerizing rhythm. Andrew wondered if he was reciting lines from one of his movies. He tried to speak, to tell him that love is more than just a word. But he couldn't open his mouth. He felt the woman's hand moving up to his chest.

"A real war is coming," Jack said. "No more of this pussy shit. And you know who's going to survive it? The ones with courage will. The ones who've seen the dark side and embraced it. They're the ones who are the most honest. Because we all have a dark side. And if you don't let it out, it will kill you."

Andrew tried to open his eyes, but they felt weighted now, sealed shut. He tried to respond to Jack, but still couldn't form any words. The woman began to caress his temples and the room seemed to be slowly turning. He saw himself in a tunnel, falling through it, the mouth of it getting smaller and farther away. The last thing he heard was Francis saying, "That's right, my captain honey. That's right."

He woke on his back, on the floor. The woman who had been sitting beside him was gone. So were Gwendolyn and Francis and Carlos. Some of the candles had burned out and the music from downstairs had stopped. Andrew could hear hysterical laughter coming from the hallway outside the room. He couldn't tell if it belonged to a man or a woman.

"Andy, my boy."

Andrew looked over at the couch and saw Jack sitting on it, alone. Jack stood and looked down at him. His fingers began to twitch at his sides and this spooked Andrew a little.

"What?" he said.

"I want your soul, Andrew."

"My what?"

"Your soul. Give it to me."

Andrew propped himself on his elbows.

"Who do you think you are? Satan?" he said.

"You don't think I am?" Jack said. "You don't think I have what it takes?"

"I think you're nuts. That's what I think."

"They say that about every genius."

Andrew tried to get up. Jack planted his foot on his chest and pushed him back down.

"I can give you the kind of life I have, Andrew."

"That's great, Jack. I think I'm still a little groggy here."

"Well, wake up and smell the coffee, man. You can have what you always wanted; power, money, women. Everything you've been dreaming about your whole miserable life."

"I'm dreaming about going home right now, if I'm not dreaming already."

"I've chosen *you*, Andrew."

"I appreciate that, Jack. Can you give me a ride? I don't feel like hitchhiking this time."

Andrew rubbed his eyes, hoping Jack would disappear by the time he finished. His head felt light in contrast to the rest of his body.

"You don't get it, do you?" Jack said.

"What was that pill you gave me?"

"A truth serum to make you stop lying to yourself. If you still believe that crap about the nobility of the working man, you're more deluded than I thought you were."

Andrew shook his head, but that didn't clear it much.

"I never said anything about the working man. Listen, I have to get out of here. I have to go home."

He tried to stand again, but Jack pushed him back down, harder this time.

"You don't know who I am, do you?" Jack said.

"Before I passed out, you were Jack Hawker. I don't know who the fuck you are now."

"You got it right before, Andrew. I'm Satan, the devil."

"Did you take one of those pills, too?"

"You don't believe me, do you?"

"I believe you're absolutely bonkers. I also believe I'll be heading back to my old life, if you don't mind."

"Is that what you really want, Andrew, to get the runaround from fish for the rest of your days? To drink cheap beer every night until you're too old to hold your glass? To marry that bar wench at Moran's?"

Andrew had stopped listening to Jack's diatribe. He'd started to think about his mother and father, for some reason, what they might think if they were alive and could see him now. He thought about Charlie and Annie, too, and wondered if they would even recognize him.

"Why do you care about me?" he said.

"Because you have potential, believe it or not."

"But you don't even know me."

"I know you better than you think I do." Jack sat on the couch again and meshed his fingers behind his head. "Take me, for example. You think I was always Jack Hawker, famous movie star? Fuck no. I was born Jason Hawkins, a fag name if there ever was one. I was raised in a trailer park in Patoka, Illinois, the kind that gets hit by tornados. My father used to beat the tar out of me and my mother didn't give a damn whether I lived or died. But that didn't stop me. In fact, it probably helped. That's why I don't cut any slack to slackers. Losers can get lost as far as I'm concerned."

Andrew closed his eyes and tried to pass out again.

"Don't try to escape into dreamland, Andrew," Jack said. "You can't keep running away."

Andrew opened his eyes. There was a piece of paper in Jack's hand now. Jack floated the paper toward him and it landed on his chest.

"What is it?"

"It's a contract. You sign it and Seth Donahue's role in *Hamptons* is yours."

"You are joking, right? I can't act."

"You don't have to. You're the real thing, remember?"

"This is crazy."

"It's not crazy at all."

Andrew rubbed his eyes again.

"And what's all that stuff about Satan?"

"Who the hell knows?" Jack shrugged, then smiled, with a hint of pity. "Jesus might love you, Andy boy. I'm sure everyone else thinks you're a loser. If I were you, I'd sign the contract."

CHAPTER 14

Karla sat on the other side of John Meade's desk and watched her editor-in-chief peering out his office window, down forty-five floors to the traffic on Madison Avenue. They looked like matchbox cars from here, nearly half of them cabs. She knew John used to drive a cab during college breaks back in the early Seventies. He'd mentioned that to her several times, describing how he would hunt fares along Madison Avenue, smug in the knowledge that he would be a fare on Madison himself one day, working in one of the glass towers he drove past. Karla never quite understood this sentimental attachment John had to the time when he was a nobody. She'd always tried her best to forget her own such days.

John had once told Karla he might be better off still driving a cab. "At least I made an honest living then," he admitted in this rare moment of candor. Occasionally, he reminded Karla that *Boulevard Magazine* used to be a quality publication, that his first job on it back in the good old days was copy editing. He had felt lucky to be making fifteen thousand just out of college. The staff writers and editors were gods to him, and *Boulevard* was the top of the heap then, the class of its class. *New York Magazine* couldn't hold a candle to it in terms of quality. The stuffy old *New Yorker* viewed it with suspicion and fear. Those were the days, John would lament, before MTV and Jerry Springer. Before the WWF and Howard Stern. American culture was taking a nosedive now, hard and fast. That's how John saw it. Karla thought he was losing his mind.

John spun his chair around.

"How was your weekend, Karla? Fun in the sun?"

"It's not fun, John. It's my job, remember?"

"Oh, yeah. I forgot."

"And how was your weekend, John? Do anything interesting?"

"We visited a couple of colleges with Jennifer. We're trying to figure out which one's going to get the rest of my money in the fall."

"Ever consider state schools?"

"State schools are for other people's kids, not mine. What's the column looking like?"

"I think I have a pretty good one. The lead item is Jack Hawker was spotted receiving, shall we say, oral pleasure from guess who?"

"I couldn't even begin to guess."

"Simone Tropper."

"Oh, Christ."

"The best part is it was at Simone and Dean's Memorial Day party. An unnamed source spotted them in the window of one of the upstairs rooms."

John spun his chair and looked out the window again. Karla could see him shaking his head ever so slightly. Dreaming about driving a cab again, John? she thought. She couldn't stand these meetings with him. She considered them to be completely unnecessary, even harmful to the integrity of her column. Without John holding her back, she knew she would really be able to let loose. Readers buy *Boulevard* for my column, John, in case you didn't know. Get with the program. Our readers feel good knowing the rich and famous are fuck-ups, too.

John faced her again.

"That happened over a month ago," he said. "Why didn't it go in the June column?"

"I decided to save it for mid-summer. Feed them smaller scandals before bringing out the big dirt."

"You're not planning to name any names, I hope."

"I never do."

"And I don't want any personal descriptions to be too vivid. No dead giveaways. You walk a pretty thin line at times as far as that's concerned."

Karla stiffened.

"Do you know why people read my column, John?"

"I'm well aware of why people read your column."

"Then why don't you let me do what I do?"

"I have to keep you within certain boundaries," John said. "That's my job."

Karla pointed the end of her Tiffany pen at her editor-in-chief.

"Let me explain something to you," she said. "I was going to wait until we sat down in September, but I'll remind you now that *Boulevard*'s circulation has shot up five hundred percent since I came onboard four years ago. I don't think that's a coincidence."

"Neither do I."

"And some of the money I bring in ends up in your pocket. If it wasn't for me, your kids would probably have to go to state schools whether you liked it or not."

John took a deep breath and waited several seconds before responding.

"Look, Karla, I don't particularly like Dean Tropper," he said. "He's a crude, obnoxious, greedy sonofabitch, as far as I'm concerned. But I'm not going to sit here and let you publicly humiliate him for no reason other than to boost your career and our circulation. I just won't do it."

Karla crossed her legs, opening the slit running more than halfway up her thigh.

"I said I'm not naming names," she said. "I never do."

"You may as well be. Everyone's going to know."

Karla smiled. John didn't smile back.

"This is a big story, John. What would the suits think if someone else got it first? What if that prick Jones over at the *Post* reported this same story and we didn't? How would that make us look?"

"It would make us look like the classier publication, which is what we were when I started here back in the Stone Age."

"Class. So passé."

"I guess you're right, if passé means it no longer exists."

"You're a hopeless romantic, John. You know that?"

John let out a short breath.

"I used to be. But I still have a few values left."

"It's all relative, you know."

"Unfortunately, I think you're right. What else do you have?"

Karla flipped open her notepad.

"I heard a rumor that Don and Melanie may drop their respective spouses and get back together."

"Sounds farfetched."

"I said it was a rumor."

"Just make that clear. Rumor. What else?"

Karla flipped the page.

"Allen Balford, that shameless worm, is angling for Seth Donahue's part in the Jack Hawker movie, no pun intended."

"How do you know?"

"He told me. But what I didn't tell *him* is I've heard they're probably going to get an unknown for the part."

John gave Karla a bored, who-gives-a-shit look.

"If you insist," he said. "Next."

"You know that blonde I spotted Ivan Wilton with? The maitre d' at Billy Starr's told me she's a call girl."

"So what?"

"It might turn into something interesting."

"That depends on your definition of interesting. Anything else?"

"The usual stuff. Who wore what. What who said. I'm going to keep an eye on Jack Hawker this summer. I'm sure there's going to be lots of dirt on that set."

"I have no doubt. Are we done here?"

"It's going to be a good column, John."

"That's what worries me."

Karla got up and made for the door, but turned before leaving.

"Oh, I nearly forgot. I'm going to need more money."

"I thought we were discussing your contract in September."

"I'm talking about petty cash."

"You mean bribe money. Christ. Go talk to Herb in accounting. The less I know about that, the better."

Karla turned to go again.

"And that Tropper thing," John said, just as she reached the door. "Heavily disguised. You hear me?"

Karla left and John sat staring across his office for a minute. Then he turned to the window and looked down at the cabs again.

CHAPTER

15

Chad made no effort to hide the fullness of his gym bag from Penny. She'll find out what's in it soon enough, he thought. He put it on the floor next to her bed and glanced over at the plant where he had hidden the camera. He could just barely see the lens through the tangle of leaves. Penny stepped out of the bathroom in her robe, rubbing a towel through her wet hair.

"Why'd you shower?" Chad said. "We're about to work out."

"I feel so dirty today. You know how some days you feel dirtier than others?"

Penny went back into the bathroom and turned on the hair drier. She shouted something Chad couldn't hear above the noise and emerged minutes later wearing a purple leotard. She hopped on the stationary bike, set it on the lowest resistance, and began to pedal.

"I thought we'd do dumbbells today," Chad said.

"Oh, I can't stand dumbbells. And I don't want to end up looking like one of those bodybuilder women."

"Don't worry. You won't."

Normally Chad would have fought her more. He felt

beyond that now. I'll be calling the shots soon enough, he thought.

"It was hot today," Penny said. "I hate hot weather."

"So do I."

Chad sat on the bed and tried to run it all through his mind. Not much to run through, really. He felt as if he'd arrived at a turning point, the kind you come to only a few times in your life. He looked at Penny pedaling at the equivalent of five miles an hour. He thought it wouldn't bother him in the slightest if he never saw her again. That didn't surprise him. What did was the realization that he felt the same way about almost anyone else he knew. He imagined making a whole new set of acquaintances, starting over completely fresh. He imagined having new parents, too, even though he was well past the point of needing parents.

"I had lunch with my friend Betsy Klein at Barn today," Penny said. "She's interested in hiring a personal trainer. I recommended you."

"I don't think I want to take on any new clients right now."

"One more won't kill you, Chad. I'm sure you can use the money."

"That's true, but I'm interested in doing other things."

"You mean that screenplay you've been telling me about? If you want my opinion, Chad, I'd stick to training. You're very good at it. All that movie business stuff is such a long shot."

"It's not such a long shot if you have contacts."

Penny gave him a scolding look.

"I told you, Francis is very busy right now," she said. "I hardly ever see him myself."

The cordless phone on the night table rang.

"Could you bring it to me, Chad?"

Chad brought her the phone.

"Hello . . . oh hi, Simone, how are you? . . . Uh huh . . . Uh huh . . . And how's Dean doing? That's good . . . Uh huh

. . . Sure, I think the kids would love to. I'll have to ask them, though. You can never tell what they'll want to do. By the way, are you looking for a personal trainer, by any chance? Because mine is really good." She looked at Chad and gave him a lewd smile. "Okay . . . Okay . . . I'll give him your number . . . fine . . . Very good. I'll talk to the kids and call you later. Bye, Simone."

Penny handed the phone back to Chad, who returned it to its cradle.

"That was Simone Tropper. She wants a play date for the kids. Get them out of our hair for a day. I tell you, summer is tough on mothers."

"Ten more minutes on the bike, then we'll do some stretches," Chad said, not wanting to hear about Penny's domestic affairs. He began to feel a bit nervous about what he planned to do, even though he knew he could forget the whole thing if he wanted to. No one was forcing him. He tried to feel some anger at Penny. After all, he had just told her he didn't want new clients and she went and recommended him to Simone Tropper. But he couldn't conjure anything more than slight annoyance. He compared it to feeling angry at a baby for crying. He likened himself to a lion stalking a deer. Lions don't feel anger toward the deer they're about to kill. They do what they need to do. That image stuck in his mind. I'm a lion. She's a deer. I'm doing what I need to do.

When Penny finished riding the bike, Chad pulled the exercise mat from under the bed. Penny lay on it and Chad put her through the stretch routine they'd devised. He did most of the work, as usual, pushing and pulling her limbs, twisting her into various contortions designed to lengthen her muscles and ligaments. Penny closed her eyes and let her body go limp. Chad decided to stretch her a little harder than he normally did. That usually got her in the mood. He put her left leg over his shoulder and leaned it forward until it had gone well past a ninety degree angle.

"Ow, Chad! That hurts."

"It's supposed to hurt."

He released her leg and Penny smiled.

"Is it really supposed to hurt?"

"There's no benefit if it doesn't. You know, no pain, no gain."

"No pain, no pleasure."

"Something like that."

"Hurt me some more, Chad."

Chad stretched her right leg to the same angle, then switched back to her left leg, bent it and pushed her knee up toward her chin. He made sure to put all his weight on her and he leaned down until his face hovered only inches above hers. He breathed a little more heavily. He knew that turned her on. Penny had opened her eyes and Chad looked directly into them. She liked that, too.

"Ow!" Penny said, half-heartedly.

"I'm not hurting you too bad, am I?"

"Just enough to make it good for me."

"Aren't you glad I forced you to do your stretches today?"

"Yes, I am." Penny's voice sounded a bit hollow now.

Chad switched back to her other leg and leaned down closer, as if preparing to kiss her. He put his hand on her throat to make her feel even more vulnerable.

"I've planned a little treat today, Penny," he said, in a firm sex game tone.

"A treat?"

"For me, that is. It's all about what I want. Isn't that right?"

"That's right."

"You're just the object of my desire. I take my pleasure from you."

"Take it, please."

Chad let go of her leg.

"Get on the bed now, Penny. Come on. Obey."

Penny immediately removed her leotard. She went over to the bed, lay on her stomach, and wiggled her ass in anticipation. Chad went to his gym bag and took out the leather mask he'd purchased at Pleasure Treasures in Greenwich Village. He put it on and zipped it down the back of his head. He felt safe turning on the camera now that his identity had been concealed.

"Don't move, Penny," he said. "If you do, I'll have to punish you."

Penny lay still and Chad tip-toed over to the plant. He quietly pressed the "Record" button on the camera, then came back to the bed and took a ball gag from his bag. He sat on Penny's back.

"What are you doing to me, Chad?"

"You'll see."

He grabbed a handful of her hair and gently lifted her head off the pillow. He slipped the gag beneath her face and inserted the ball into her mouth. He tied the straps behind her head.

"Can you breath okay?"

Penny nodded. Chad took the leather bustier from his bag next.

"Now I want you to put this on, Penny. I think you'll look extremely sexy in it."

Penny got off the bed and began to laugh when she saw Chad in the mask.

"What's so funny, bitch?"

Penny stopped laughing and put on the bustier. Chad handed her a pair of crotchless panties.

"Put these on, too."

Penny did, her eyes open wide—with excitement, not fear. Chad took out a length of nylon rope.

"Get back on the bed," he said. "I want you on your hands and knees."

Chad guided her so she faced the camera. He knelt on the bed behind her and tied her hands behind her back. He reached into the bag once again and pulled out a cat-o-nine-tails. He flicked its tentacles across her back.

"You've been a very bad girl, Penny Baskin." He spoke loudly, enunciating each word clearly, but keeping his voice in its sleazy sex tone so it wouldn't be easily recognized. Penny nodded and murmured, looking directly into the camera without knowing it.

"You've been bad and lazy and insulting, Penny Baskin," Chad continued. "You haven't thought about others or appreciated all you have. You're going to be severely punished for that."

Chad whipped her again, a little harder this time. Penny let out a muffled yelp. Chad smacked her butt with his hand, then pulled her hair again, tilting her head back to make sure the camera got good view of her face. He whipped her with the cat-o-nine-tails once more.

"Do you like being humiliated like this, Penny Baskin?"

Penny nodded and murmured something unintelligible.

"Do you like being fucked by strange men, Penny?"

Penny nodded again.

"Is that because your husband, Francis Baskin, no longer fucks you?"

Penny groaned.

"And is it true that Francis no longer fucks you because he prefers to fuck men?"

Penny nodded and wiggled her ass and said something indecipherable through the ball gag.

"What was that, Penny? Oh, you want me to fuck you now? Beg me."

Penny squealed.

"Louder."

Penny did.

"Okay. I'm cruel but fair."

Chad dropped his shorts. He wasn't wearing any underwear today. He didn't have to stroke himself to get hard, or conjure up his usual fantasy. This seemed close enough to it. He placed his hands firmly on both sides of Penny's rear and pulled her back onto him. She was already soaked and he slid into her easily. Penny groaned again and Chad immediately found a rhythm, remembering to slap her butt and use the cat-o-nine-tails every once in a while. He untied the gag and tried to recall lines from another porn movie he'd been in.

"Is this what you want or is this what you need, Penny?" he said, finally remembering one.

"It's what I need," Penny gasped. "It's what I want and what I need."

"I guess you always get what you want, don't you? Money can buy anything, can't it?"

Penny didn't answer. She was too busy coming. She let out a scream, then began to weep. That should be sufficient, Chad thought, pulling out of her. Penny collapsed forward onto her stomach and Chad helped her out of the bustier and the panties, then pulled the sheet over her. Within minutes, he could detect a steady rhythm to her breathing. Satisfied that she was asleep, he walked over to the plant, lifted the camera out of it, and pressed the "Stop" button. Then he took off his mask and packed the bondage gear back into his gym bag, zipping it slowly to keep from making any noise that might wake his client. Sleep tight, Penny, he thought, on his way out of the room.

PART FOUR

AUGUST

Some of the fishermen begin to catch tuna, monsters from the waters east of Montauk Point, their belly meat tender enough to cut with a fork. The days have already peaked by now, and become noticeably shorter. The sky has lost most of its luminescence, replaced by a deadening haze of humidity.

The summer people are becoming agitated, their anxiety spreading amongst them like a virus. It happens this way every August, as the summer escapes before it can be properly and thoroughly consumed. In people's minds, not enough golden days have been spent on the beach, nor has enough summer produce been eaten. Too few sunsets have been watched, and passionate sex remains elusive.

The frequency of accidents on the Montauk Highway always increases during this phase of the season. Tempers are beginning to sour, too. Fights break out at the Amagansett Farmer's Market, and some are already looking forward to cool autumn days in the city, weekends spent admiring the foliage in Central Park. Maybe I'll sink my teeth into life then, people seem to be thinking. Maybe in the fall I'll really taste it.

And off Mecox Beach in Bridgehampton, another drowning occurs. This time a ten year-old boy goes under while his mother sits reading Karla Sands' column in *Boulevard Magazine*.

CHAPTER 16

A Death In The Hamptons started filming in July and half the scenes had been shot by the middle of August, most of them in Montauk and the Springs. No one except the local reporters and gossip columnists seemed happy about the added mayhem and traffic the movie brought to the already overcrowded East End.

Not surprisingly, Andrew didn't mind it, either. He adapted to acting more readily than anyone expected. Jack had been right about him being perfect for the role, "the real thing." He played the scenes like he would normally act in real life. He found the ones on the trawler especially easy. But while in the movie his life had changed very little, the same could not be said once the cameras stopped rolling.

"Cut!" Francis yelled. "One more time!"

They were filming the scene where Andrew's character, Jed, confronts Jack's character, David, because he suspects David has designs on his wife, Mary, played by Gwendolyn. Jed and David fish together on the same boat and the tension building between them had been causing Jed to drink even more heavily. This pushes Mary further into David's arms. The crew couldn't stop talking about how great the script was, even though every one of them knew it sucked. But they all wanted to work on Francis's next film. This kind of self-interested flattery is common on movie sets.

Andrew walked back to his mark and faced Jack again. Francis yelled "Action!" and Andrew repeated his lines:

"She doesn't care about you. She never did. I'm her husband. I'm the one she loves."

Jack smiled slyly and said his line:

"If you say so, big guy."

"Cut!"

Francis stepped from behind his cinematographer and came over to Andrew and Jack. He had reverted back to manly mode. He never lost it on the set.

"How we doing, chief?" Jack said to him.

"Brilliant, as always." Francis turned to Andrew. "Andrew Kane, the Natural. No training. Just pure instinct. I love it."

"Give me the lines and I'll say them," Andrew said, with a modest shrug.

"Let's break for an hour, then we'll shoot the scene where Mary shows up," Francis said. "I want anger and tension in this one. Real fucking anger and real fucking tension."

Francis and Jack headed off toward the craft services truck and Andrew went back to his trailer. He found a PA waiting outside of it. He had never spoken to this one, but had noticed her clean-cut, prep school looks. He had even entertained a few passing fantasies about what might lie beneath her wholesome veneer.

"Um, Mister Kane?" she said.

"Call me Andrew."

"Okay, um, Andrew. Hi, I'm, um, Sally Dugan?"

"Are you sure?" Andrew said, imitating Lander Sobel, just for fun.

"Of course, I'm sure."

"You said it as a question. What can I do for you, Sally Dugan?"

"Well, nothing really. I just wanted to tell you I think you're really talented and um, well I was wondering if I could maybe talk to you for a few minutes, maybe ask you some questions. I don't want to bother you on your break, but I was—"

"Come on in. We can talk inside."

Andrew opened the door of his trailer and checked out Sally's ass as she stepped up into it. Not bad, he thought, not bad at all.

"You want a drink, Sally?"

"A Coke would be fine, thanks."

Andrew took one from the refrigerator and a Heineken for himself. He gave Sally the Coke and motioned for her to sit on the couch. He sat on the love seat across from her. She's a young one, he thought, looking her over, no more than twenty. Easy pickings, most likely. He knew his stare was making Sally nervous. He kept staring anyway and decided to continue his Lander Sobel routine, to see how far he could go with it.

"Tell me about yourself, Sally."

"Well, I'm in film school at NYU."

"And how'd you get this job?"

"My dad knows Francis. They grew up together in Maryland."

"So you want to make movies one day?"

"Yup. It's what I've wanted to do since I was little."

"That's nice. Most kids don't know what they want to do with themselves. It's good to have goals, even ones that are almost impossible to reach."

This made Sally pause. Her brow scrunched.

"I don't think anything's impossible if you put your mind to it," she said. "Look at you. You landed a major role in a movie and you've never acted before."

"But I had to sell my soul to the devil."

Sally giggled, then looked down at her feet for a moment

before looking up again.

"But really, I don't think anything is impossible if you want it badly enough," she said.

"Why do you want to make films so badly?"

"Well, I guess because films are sort of the great American art form."

Andrew fixed her with the same unnerving stare.

"Is that something you learned in one of your classes?"

"No. Well, yes. But I think it's true."

"Most films these days are terrible. You should know that."

"That doesn't mean you can't make a good and meaningful one."

"And who's going to want to distribute your good and meaningful film if you ever scrape up enough money to actually make it?"

Sally looked out the window of the trailer and seemed ready to cry. Go on and cry, Andrew thought, shocked and a little scared by how mean he felt, and by how good he was at this game Lander had played on him not long ago.

"I disagree," Sally said. "There's always going to be an audience for good films, just like there'll always be people who read good books."

Andrew crossed his legs and rested his ankle on his knee.

"You're probably right about that," he said. "But what makes you think you can make a good film?"

"I know I can."

"Because your daddy spent a lot of money to send you to NYU film school? Because your daddy got you a job here on the set?"

"Why are you being so mean?"

Andrew feigned innocence.

"I'm not being mean, Sally. I just don't see it happening for you. I'm trying to save you the trouble of having to find out for yourself, that's all."

Sally seemed ready to cry again.

"You're not trying to save me any trouble," she said. "I don't know why I'm still even talking to you."

"Because you like me."

"How could I possibly like you after what you just said?"

"What I meant is you're attracted to me. It's not your fault. You can't help it."

Sally stood and made for the door.

"You're an asshole," she said.

"Aren't you going to thank me, Sally? I did give you some good advice."

The corners of Sally's mouth turned down.

"Fuck you, Andrew," she said. "I hope you never get another role for as long as you live."

She left the trailer, slamming the door behind her. Andrew kept his eyes on it, half expecting Sally to come back, either to apologize or express more outrage. She didn't, so he put his feet up on the coffee table and drank his Heineken. He didn't feel especially good or bad about what he'd said to Sally, just perplexed. Because he had no idea why he'd done it, particularly since things were going well for him. So well that he could no longer imagine how he ever lived the way he used to: broke and burdened, bored and frustrated. He tried to feel how he felt back then, and remember what he used to think about. It all seemed to be fading so quickly, as if even his recent past belonged to someone else. Fuckit, he thought. He picked up the *Hamptons* shooting script and began to read the next scene:

EXT. MONTAUK DOCK-DAY

JED and DAVID continue unloading fish from their boat. Neither is talking to each other after their argument about MARY. Then MARY pulls up in the car. She gets out and approaches them.

                    MARY
        Hi fellas. Catch much today?

                    JED
              (not looking up)
          Not much.

                   MARY
              (forcing cheerfulness)
          Don't worry. I'm sure you'll
          catch more tomorrow.

                    JED
          What makes you say that?

                   MARY
          I just have a feeling.

                    JED
          I wish it was that easy, just
          having a feeling about every-
          thing.

David notices the hurt look on Mary's face.

                   DAVID
          Why don't you ease up on her,
          Jed?

Jed flashes an angry look at David.

                    JED
          Why don't you mind your own
          business, David? She's my
          wife, unless you forgot
          already.

                   DAVID
          She might be your wife, but
          that doesn't mean she wants to
          be with you.
                    JED
          You're living in a dream world.

                         DAVID
          Ask her, Jed.

                          JED
          I'm not going to ask her any-
          thing.

     David turns to Mary, who stands there,
     unsure what to do.

                         DAVID
          Tell him, Mary. Tell him I'm
          the one you want to be with.
          I'm the one you always wanted
          to be with.

     Tears have begun to drip down Mary's
     cheeks.

                    DAVID (CONT'D)
          Go on, Mary. Tell him.

     Mary turns to Jed, who eagerly awaits
     her answer.

     I couldn't write worse if I tried, Andrew thought. Someone
knocked on his door and said, "Ten minutes, Mr. Kane."
     Andrew finished the scene, then his beer, then went back
out onto the set.
     "What did you do to that poor PA, Andrew?" Jack said.
"A little rough riding?"
     "Nothing too rough."
     Jack chuckled and slapped Andrew's back.
     "I've created a monster. I love it."
     Francis and the cinematographer were already setting up
the shot. Andrew went over and watched them work. He
thought through his lines and envisioned the scene. He tried
to decide what tone he should use when challenging
Gwendolyn's character to proclaim her love for his character,
not Jack's. Yeah, this movie bites the big one, he thought. It
doesn't matter, though. It'll be a hit.

✛

They went to Rocket that night after eating at Sasha and Joe's. Andrew drove them in the new Mercedes SUV Jack had lent him. They arrived a little after 11pm and people had already gathered outside the club. Jack led Gwendolyn and Andrew through the crowd, pushing club-goers out of his way until he got to the front. The doorman shook his hand and let the three of them in.

The club was jammed inside as well, house music blaring, lights flashing, glammed-out people dancing with each other, but mainly with themselves. Some of the patrons sat at tables on the perimeter, sharing bottles of champagne and vodka, watching everyone else. Jack led Gwendolyn and Andrew across the dance floor to the VIP lounge in the back. The waitress gave them a corner table and Jack ordered a bottle of champagne and three glasses.

The champagne arrived and Andrew spotted Sugar B at the table next to theirs. Tonight, his posse consisted of three women, two black and one white, and the same two toughs. They were drinking champagne, too, and everyone was laughing except for Sugar B. He looked over at Andrew and a Mona Lisa smile lifted the corners of his mouth ever so slightly. He raised his glass, a slow, deliberate gesture. Andrew toasted him back.

People came to the table, stayed a while, then left. Andrew couldn't keep track of them. He didn't bother anymore. He'd been to Rocket with Jack and Gwendolyn several times before and now knew that staying disengaged was the best way. A photographer took a picture of Jack and Gwendolyn. Before he could leave the table, Jack asked for his camera, pretending to be interested in its make. The photographer gave it to him and Jack threw it to the floor, smashing it into several pieces.

"I don't like my picture being taken," Jack said.

— 146 —

While the photographer gathered the remains of his camera, Andrew eyed the women at the other tables. A small, greasy-looking man he recognized came over.

"It's going to be fucking great," he said, the words shooting like bullets from his mouth, his eyes darting around the room as he spoke. "The movie. Fucking great. Blow, anyone?"

Jack put out his index finger and the man immediately tapped some cocaine from a vial onto it. Jack brought it to his nose and inhaled. Gwendolyn took some, too, then Andrew. Nothing needed to be concealed in Rocket's VIP room.

"It's good shit," the man said. "Good, good shit. I can get as much as you want if you want."

"Why buy it when I can get it for free?" Jack said.

"Well, when the favors stop coming, you know where to find me. I'm always here. You know that, right?"

The man left the table and went over to Sugar B's. He affected African-American mannerisms.

"Hey, Sugar B. Wassup, my man?"

"Sugar B?" Sugar B said. "It's Z-Best now."

"You changed your name again?"

"And don't forget it, asshole."

"Z-Best. I like it. I like it a lot. Want some blow, Z-Best? Good shit."

"I got enough for now."

"When you run dry, you come to me, blood. I'm the one who cares."

The dealer moved on to a table of European-looking models. Andrew watched him work, pleased that he hadn't lied about the quality of his product. The coke hit him fast and hard, immediately speeding his thoughts and whetting his appetites. He'd found them to be insatiable lately. Like a shark, he now needed to feed them constantly, always wanting more than what he had. As he scanned the room for something interesting, the sight of Pete Moran standing at the entrance jolted him. He hadn't spoken to Pete since the week he found Seth Donahue's body. Their eyes met and Andrew suddenly felt ashamed to be here, as if he had somehow failed Pete.

Pete approached the table.

"I'm surprised to see you here, Pete," Andrew said.

"A couple of months ago I might have said the same about you." Pete sat. "I was searching for you and Jack Hawker. Looks like my lucky night."

Andrew introduced Pete to Jack and Gwendolyn.

"Don't want to take up much of your time," Pete said. "I just want to ask you guys a few questions about Seth Donahue."

"I'll be happy to help any way I can," Jack said. "Seth was a good friend of mine."

"Sorry to hear that. I understand Seth was going to be in the movie you're filming."

"That's right." Jack winked at Andrew. "But I think we got a pretty good replacement."

Pete looked at Andrew and couldn't help smiling.

"The good Lord takes from some and gives to others." He looked at Jack again. "Is there anyone you can think of who had even the slightest motive to kill Donahue? Any enemies? Did he have a falling out with a friend or get in an argument with someone that you know of?"

Jack shook his head, and seemed to become genuinely sad.

"Sheriff, I've been trying to think of something since it happened. He didn't have an enemy in the world, as far as I know."

"That's what I hear."

"It's always the nice guys who get it," Jack said.

"Not always, but usually." Pete pulled a pad from his back pocket and made a few notes in it. He turned to Andrew. "Is there anything else you can remember, Andrew? What about the currents? Do you happen to remember which way were they flowing that morning?"

"Why?"

"That might help me figure out where the body came from."

The waitress asked Pete if he wanted a drink. Pete told her no thanks and his eyes lingered on her legs as she walked away.

"You like that, Sheriff?" Jack said.

"Who wouldn't? So about the currents, Andrew."

"I think they were running northeast. They usually do that time of year."

"That would make sense. You found him off Montauk, so he was probably killed somewhere in the Hamptons. That's fairly obvious. Anything else?"

"Not that I can think of. So I heard it was a machete."

Pete let out a tired breath.

"I just hope he was already dead before he got butchered." He made a few more notes before closing the pad. "Well, I better get going. This kind of place makes me feel my age."

"Why don't you stick around, sheriff," Jack said. "It might take a few years off."

"The way the world is headed, I'm starting to think that might not be such a good thing." Pete handed Jack his card. "If you think of anything, give me a call."

"I will, sheriff."

"And take care of Andrew, here. He's not used to this kind of life."

"Oh, he's learning fast, Sheriff. Real fast."

Pete patted Andrew's shoulder, then left. Jack watched the door until he was gone.

"Well, that was a real mood killer," he said. "We need some more white stuff to get this party going again."

Andrew grudgingly agreed. Although he had always liked Pete, his visit had reminded him of the body, as well as his former life. He drank some more champagne, but it couldn't completely counter the depression he felt coming on. A woman he'd never met came over and sat on his lap. The woman had a round, moonlike face and big, blue eyes. Beside that, she looked similar to the countless, nameless others he'd been meeting almost every night.

"I hear you're good," the woman said. "That's what I hear."

"Did I invite you sit on my lap?"

"I couldn't resist."

Andrew rested his hand on her bare thigh.

"What do you have for me?" he said.

"What do you want?"

Good question, Andrew thought.

"Tell me how good I am," he said.

"I just did."

"Tell me I'm great, then."

The woman leaned close to him.

"I hear you're great," she said. "Aren't you going to ask my name?"

"Why should I?"

"That way we can get to know each other."

Andrew sipped some champagne. He looked over at Jack, snorting a cocaine sample from another dealer. Gwendolyn was laughing at something a man in a tailored red suit said to her.

"What is it?" Andrew said.

"Clover."

"Is that a real name?"

Clover poked Andrew's chest with her finger.

"That was obnoxious. Clover's a real name. I'm for real, you know."

Andrew looked at her breasts.

"Sure you are," he said.

Clover draped her arms around his neck.

"Do they need any extras on the set, Andrew?"

Andrew decided to do what Jack would in this situation.

"If you give me a kiss, they might."

Clover kissed his lips.

"Do they?" she said.

"I don't think so."

Clover kissed him again.

"Are you sure?"

 "Maybe if you give me more than a kiss."

"Here?"

"Not here."

✝

They left Jack and Gwendolyn at Rocket and drove to Clover's house, a suburban-looking affair on Gibson Lane in Bridgehampton. Clover and five of her friends had rented it for the summer. Each had a separate room and Clover took Andrew to hers.

"What do you do?" Andrew asked, sitting on her bed. He really didn't care.

"I do sales for a clothing designer in the garment district. Kleinman-Sandler? Ever heard of them?"

"Never."

"I guess you'd have no reason to."

Clover took off her high heels and her dress. She had a girlish figure except for her disproportionately large breasts.

"Are you from out here originally?" she said.

"I've never really lived anywhere else."

Andrew didn't feel like talking about himself, so he fucked her instead, in every position he knew. It felt good, not great, and at times his mind wandered, not settling on anything for long. He forgot Clover's name for a few minutes. Then he remembered it and had to hold back a laugh. He pretended she was someone else for a while, an actress he'd seen in a movie once, the waitress at Sasha and Joe's that he found attractive. His wandering thoughts settled briefly on Ralph and Donny at Moran's. He felt guilty about not going there for so long. He thought of Katie next, and he came while thinking of her. He rolled off of Clover and let her cuddle up to him, but only for a minute. He used to like cuddling. Now it annoyed him. He got out of the bed and dressed.

"Will I see you again?" Clover said.

"I don't think so."

Andrew left the room and the house. The sun still hadn't risen and the darkness showed no sign of thinning yet. He could hear the surf in the distance. It always seemed to carry further this early. He got in the SUV, pulled out of the driveway, and soon found himself on the highway, which was completely empty. He felt angry now, not satisfied and relaxed like he knew he should. He felt frustrated and sad, too, but didn't know why. He shut off the headlights, pushed the pedal all the way down, and sped into the darkness.

CHAPTER

17

Chad decided to let Penny ride the bike for as long as she wanted. That would give him time to formulate his words, his presentation. He knew he needed to seem calm and reasonable. Anger or impatience wouldn't do. Nor would any sign of desperation. Just lay it on the line to her, as matter-of-factly as possible. He had a copy of the tape in his gym bag. He'd mailed one to a friend in New York, with instructions not to open it. He'd stashed the third in a place only he could find.

He'd waited for more than a month to finally do it. No point in rushing. He hadn't learned much in his thirty years, but he had learned to wait on things, allow time for flaws to become apparent. But after several weeks, his plan only seemed to get better. He often found himself dreaming about the money, about what he would do once he had it. The idea of using it to make his screenplay into a film had gradually lost its appeal compared to just having it, being able to spend it on whatever he wanted. Movies are a crapshoot, anyway, he told himself.

He sat on the bed and watched Penny ride. He considered putting her through some calisthenics before popping the hundred thousand dollar question. She was paying for this session, after all. She deserved the full benefit.

Then it happened. He started feeling sorry for her again. Now's not the time, he told himself. Just remember, she probably wouldn't piss on you if you caught fire. She wouldn't give you the time of day if you asked her for it. And what is she? She's not talented or smart. She's not charming or sensitive or even very nice. Without Francis, she'd be nothing.

"Another ten minutes, Penny," he said.

"Maybe I'll try to go another fifteen."

"If you feel up to it."

"I do. I feel good today."

Penny began to pedal faster and Chad saw a light sweat start to shine her skin.

"You're sweating," he said. "I've never seen you do that before."

Penny smiled, like a kid proud of performing a difficult task for the first time.

"Oh, I finally did speak to Francis about you," she said. "He says you should send your script to his assistant. I'll give you her address. I know it's not exactly what you hoped for, but it's something."

"That's nice. Thanks, Penny."

"I'm really sorry I couldn't get you a real meeting with him, but he's so busy with the movie and all."

Chad felt the bottom dropping out of his contempt for her.

"I understand," he said, meaning it. "Thanks. I appreciate it."

Dammit! he thought. She has to turn into a human being now of all times. Forget about it, Chad. You have to go through with this. It's nothing personal. Besides, no one's going to get hurt because no one will find out about it. She comes up with the money, and the only people who will ever see the tape will be me and her. Sure, I'll keep a copy, just in case, but I'll keep my word, too. I'm a man of honor. Man of honor. He liked that.

The fifteen minutes seemed to take an hour. It's a shame she didn't always work out this hard, Chad thought. But what does it matter? It's my last session with her. Hopefully it will be my last session with anyone. Let's face it, I'm not a good trainer. A good trainer cares if his clients make progress. I never did. But so what? I won't have to do this ever again, not with a hundred grand at my disposal. Maybe I *will* finance the movie with it. Movies have been made for a lot less. *The Blair Witch Project*, for example. Or maybe I'll just invest the money, play the market with it.

"Can we do that bondage thing again, Chad?"

"Bondage? I didn't bring the stuff."

"Bring it next time."

"Okay. Hey, time's up."

Penny stopped and got off the bike. Her face had acquired a healthy flush and Chad thought she actually looked sort of pretty. He'd never thought that before. Penny sat on the bed next to him.

"I wanted to thank you, Chad," she said. "For what it's worth."

"Thank me? For what?"

Penny looked him in the eye and didn't seem embarrassed by what she was about to say.

"I've begun to appreciate the fact that you make me feel like a woman. I haven't felt that way in a long time."

A sweat broke on Chad's brow despite the air-conditioning. Suddenly, Penny seemed like a different person to him, a better one. *Goddammit!*

"It's nothing, Penny," he said. "No big deal."

"Maybe not for you."

She kissed Chad's cheek and Chad sat there paralyzed— not only his body, but his brain, too.

"Well," he said. "Um."

Penny kissed him again, then got off the bed.

"Should we do dumbbells now?"

Chad sat there unable to answer, his whole plan grinding

to a halt, his future crumbling before his eyes. He pictured himself twenty years from now, still a broke trainer spending his summers in a pool house. He knew he'd come to a crucial moment, that what he did now mattered more than perhaps any other time in his life. What's it going to be, Chad? He stood and faced Penny. Why are you doing this to me? Why?

"I want to show you something, Penny."

He unzipped his bag, took out the video, then slowly walked over to the TV and turned it on. He turned on the VCR as well and flipped the TV to channel three. He hesitated before inserting the cassette, then did it and turned up the volume. He stepped aside so Penny could see.

Penny watched the entire tape without speaking or moving a muscle. Her blank expression never changed. Chad ejected the tape when it ended, and put it back in his bag. Penny seemed ready to speak, but was unable to.

"Maybe you should sit down, Penny."

Penny remained standing, still looking at the screen that had gone to snow.

"How did you do that?" she said, in a stunned monotone.

"That's not important."

"What do you plan to do with it?"

"That's what I wanted to talk to you about."

"What do you plan to do with it, Chad?"

"The good news is, I don't plan to do anything with it. You see, if you pay me a hundred grand, I'll just give it to you and you can watch it when you happen to get the itch. I actually think it's pretty good. I've seen enough of them to know."

Penny seemed completely devoid of any affect now, like a zombie.

"A hundred grand," she said, still in montone. "You mean a hundred thousand dollars."

"That's right. Cash is best, but I'll take a check." Chad hadn't thought about that particular detail. A hundred grand in cash is hard to obtain in one lump, even if you are married to Francis Baskin. And a check might raise serious suspicion on both ends of the transaction.

Penny turned to him, anger deepening her exercise flush.

"And if I refuse?" she said.

"If you refuse, there are lots of things I can do. All of them kind of involve the media. They're always looking for stuff like this. Penny Baskin, wife of famous director, Francis Baskin, caught on tape doing the nasty with someone other than Francis, who is revealed to be gay. You guys are high profile. People would be interested."

Penny took a step toward Chad. Chad took a step back and picked up the gym bag.

"How do I know you won't sell it to the media even if I do pay you?" Penny said. "I'm sure that's not your only copy. You're stupid, but not that stupid."

That last comment hurt. And the fact that Penny seemed to have gathered her wits only made Chad more nervous. He tried to lighten the situation with a smile.

"I wouldn't do that, Penny," he said. "I'm a man of my word. I mean, I'm a man of honor."

"You're a piece of shit. That's what you are. I should have you arrested."

"For what?"

"Extortion, schmuck."

"It would be your word against mine."

"That's true, retard, but I think that tape would provide enough evidence of what you're up to."

Chad felt some of his confidence returning.

"But do you want the cops to see it?" he said. "How long do you think it would be before it hit the news?"

The balance of power seemingly back in his favor, Chad looked into Penny's eyes and could almost read the thoughts behind them. I got you coming and going, Penny. If we were playing chess, I'd say this is checkmate. Then Penny's mouth drew into a tight line.

"Go fuck yourself," she said, calmly.

Chad actually felt his heart dropping into his stomach.

She's not rolling over so easily, he thought.

"What do you mean by that?" he said.

"What I meant was Go. Fuck. Your. Self."

She's angry. Chad thought. But she's going to pay. Then it dawned on him that maybe she wouldn't.

"You're going to pay me the money, aren't you, Penny? The way I see it, you don't have much choice."

"GO. FUCK. YOUR. SELF!" Penny repeated. "What part of that don't you understand?"

Chad couldn't look her in the eye anymore, so he looked over at the snowy TV screen.

"Are you sure?" he said.

"Get out of here. Now."

"You're making a mistake, Penny."

"I didn't make any mistake. You did. Get out of my house."

Chad felt like crying right there and then. But he held his tears. Never let them see you cry. And never let them see you sweat, unless you're working out. These had always been two of his rules. He had others, but he couldn't remember them right now. He gave Penny a lame half-smile, as if to say "No hard feelings." Penny didn't react and Chad quickly left her room. He went directly to the pool house and within half an hour, he'd packed his things into his suitcase and moved out. He knew a Plan B would have to be formulated. But first he needed to figure out where to spend the night.

CHAPTER
18

Donny pounded his fist on the bar.
"I can't fucking believe it!" he said, his cigarette bouncing between his lips.

Katie stopped rotating the beer bottles in the cooler.

"You been that saying that for weeks, Donny."

"That's because I still can't fucking believe it." Donny nudged Ralph with his elbow. "Can you, Ralph?"

"No, I can't."

"And it's just like I predicted," Donny continued. "He gets the part in the movie and now he don't want to know us anymore."

"He's probably been busy," Katie said.

Donny stubbed out his cigarette.

"Don't make excuses for him, Katie. I wouldn't hurt him any to come in and say hello to his old friends once in a while. Now that he's making all that dough, you'd think he'd buy us a few beers, just for old time sake."

Katie continued rotating the bottles and Donny and Ralph each went into one of their broods. "I hear he drives a brand new Mercedes SUV now," Ralph said, finally. "The kind that spoiled rich blonde girl drove into those people outside that club."

"Good for him," Donny grumbled.

"I hear he's been going to all the fancy restaurants and night clubs, too."

"That doesn't make him better than us."

"I didn't say it did. I'm just telling you what I heard."

Donny finished his beer

"I'll tell you this, Ralph. If I ever by some chance get a role in a movie, I'm not going to forget my old pal, Ralph, not unless hell freezes over."

"Thanks, Donny. Same goes for me."

"And I wouldn't go around driving hot-shot cars and eating expensive meals and going to clubs with all those assholes."

"Neither would I . . . Well, I might buy a new pickup truck. That wouldn't be bad, would it? Mine's on its last legs."

"A new pickup would be fine. Nothing wrong with that."

Katie replaced their empty bottles with full ones.

"How was the fishing today, boys?"

"Same as yesterday," Ralph said.

"I forgot to ask you yesterday."

"Yesterday sucked," Donny said.

Katie resumed rotating beer bottles. Donny and Ralph went back to brooding. Another few minutes passed before Ralph said, "Did you hear about the women?"

"What women?" Donny said.

"The ones Andrew's been with."

Katie stopped rotating the bottles. She listened more carefully.

"What's your source?" Donny said.

"Bill Strickland. Bartends down at the Red Monkey. Bill says he's seen Andrew and Jack Hawker there a bunch of times. He says Andrew always has a different girl with him."

Katie couldn't tell exactly how this made her feel. She assured herself that it couldn't be jealousy. Andrew wasn't her man, after all.

"Andrew the ladies man," Donny said.

"Never thought of him that way," Ralph said.

"A little money and fame will turn any slob into a ladies man, even you, Ralph."

Katie finished with the bottles.

"You two remind me of old ladies gossiping," she said.

"We've known Andrew our whole lives," Donny said. "Now it's like we don't even exist to him. That doesn't bother you, Katie?"

"Why should it?"

"Don't tell me you never noticed how he used to look at you."

"I never did," Katie lied.

"Gimme a break. He was in love with you. Everyone knows that. Now? He don't need love anymore."

"I hear he went to—what's that place called? Sara and Joe's," Ralph said. "I hear he went there and ordered caviar for an appetizer, the main course and dessert."

"I don't believe that," Katie said.

"Okay, I made that one up. But I hear he's been going there a lot."

"He's entitled," Katie said. "From what I read in the *Star*, he's a pretty good actor."

"Playing a fisherman?" Donny said. "Not a big stretch, if you ask me."

Tired of listening to these two, Katie went to the end of the bar and started cleaning glasses that didn't need to be cleaned. But they're right, she thought. Andrew's a bastard for not coming in, not even once. She wondered if he'd slept with any of those girls.

Donny and Ralph stayed later than they usually did, as if waiting around for their own lucky break. They shot a couple games of pool and Ralph won both. He didn't seem very happy about it, though, and Donny didn't seem to mind losing like he normally did. They came back to the bar and Katie gave them a round on the house.

Then Andrew came in. He sat on his stool and the few patrons left in Moran's eyed him, as if he had become a dangerous animal.

"Well, well, well," Donny said. "Look what we have here."

"How you been, Donny?"

Donny pulled back in mock amazement.

"Holy shit! He remembers my name."

Andrew rolled his eyes.

"It hasn't been that long."

"Not for you. I'm sure every day for you is just one big whirlwind."

Katie came over with a bottle of Budweiser.

"Hi, Andrew. Good to see you."

"Good to see you too, Katie. You know, I'll have a Heineken instead."

"Oooh! Heineken," Donny said. "Looks like Budweiser's not good enough for Andrew anymore."

"It still is. I just like Heineken better." Andrew leaned back so he could see Ralph on the other side of Donny. "How's it going, Ralph?"

"Fine. How are you?" Ralph answered quickly. He shot a glance at Andrew before averting his eyes.

"Fishing going okay, Ralph?"

"Yeah. Good."

Katie brought Andrew's Heineken.

"Thanks, Katie. Good seeing you."

"We were wondering when you'd be coming in," Katie said.

"I've been meaning to. It's been real busy. The movie and all."

Katie tapped her forehead, with pretend forgetfulness.

"Oh, yeah, the movie," she said. "How's it coming?"

"Movies are movies. You know."

"No, we don't know," Donny broke in. "We don't make movies like you do."

"Maybe you should, Donny. It pays better than fishing."

"Whoa. You don't hold back any, do you?"

"Neither do you."

Donny turned away from Andrew, not all the way, but enough to indicate his disgust. Andrew looked at Katie again and winked.

"You look good, Katie."

"Listen to Don Juan here," Donny mumbled to Ralph.

"Thanks," Katie said, wishing she had taken the time to fix her hair tonight, put on some makeup. She didn't know what else to say and she could feel the weight of Andrew's stare, his eyes roaming her body, not just her face. She went to the register and pretended to sort through some delivery receipts. Donny tapped Andrew's shoulder.

"Can I have your autograph, Mr. Kane?"

"Donny, Donny, Donny. What am I going to do with you? Let me buy you and Ralph a beer."

"We thought you'd never ask. I'll have a Heineken, if you don't mind."

Andrew bought a Heineken for Donny and a Budweiser for Ralph. He knew Ralph would never try a Heineken.

"So, you been banging a lot of chicks, Andrew?" Donny said, after Katie delivered the beers and returned to the register.

"I've been getting my share."

"That must be nice," Ralph said, staring straight ahead.

"To tell you the truth, it gets a little tiring after a while."

"Sounds like hell," Donny said. "Pure hell."

Andrew looked at Katie by the register. She had her back turned, giving him the view he wanted.

"The problem is, the more you get, the more you want," he said.

"Oh, boo hoo." Donny elbowed Ralph. "Boo hoo. Right, Ralph?"

"Yeah, boo hoo," Ralph parroted, half-heartedly. He still couldn't look at Andrew.

"It's like as soon as you get the girl you've been wanting,

you want a different one," Andrew continued. "And as soon as you get that one, it's on to the next."

"Well, if you ever want to throw one of your leftovers my way, don't hesitate," Donny said

"But you're married."

"So? Look at the Europeans. You're practically a queer over there if you don't have something on the side."

"I'll keep you in mind, Donny."

"Yeah, sure you will."

Andrew had been looking at Katie the whole time. When she turned around, he said, "You want to have dinner with me, Katie?"

"I work nights, remember?"

"What night are you off?"

"Wednesdays. You know that."

"That's right. Wednesdays. So we'll do it Wednesday. That all right with you?"

Katie shrugged.

"Sure. Why not?"

Andrew stood and went to the bathroom. Donny was gone when he returned, his half full Heineken still on the bar.

"Where did Donny go, Ralph?"

"He went home."

"Why?"

Ralph turned his palms up, then began to peel the label off his Budweiser bottle. "Say, Andrew. I was, well . . . I was thinking that—"

"Hey Ralph, don't be so nervous. It's just me."

"I know, but now you're an actor and all. Anyway, I was thinking. Well, you know my old pickup?"

"What about it?"

"It's kind of . . . you know, it's old and beat up and all. The transmission's nearly shot."

"That's too bad. I always liked that truck. What year is it, again?"

"Eighty-Three."

"It'll be a classic pretty soon."

"I don't think it's going to make it that long."

"That's why they call them classics. Not many make it."

Ralph drank some beer for courage and looked directly at Andrew for the first time.

"Andrew, could you give me a loan?" It came out quickly, the only way he could do it. He faced forward again.

"A loan?" Andrew said.

"So I can buy a new truck. I hate to ask you, I really do, but I don't know what I'll do if it breaks down. I'll pay you back, with interest if you want."

Andrew didn't respond right away. He already knew his answer, but preferred to make Ralph wait for it. He could feel that still-unfamiliar meanness welling inside of him again. He wondered if it had always been there and was finally coming to the surface after so many years. Maybe it's Jack Hawker rubbing off on me, he thought. Maybe Jack really *is* Satan. Or maybe it's Lander Sobel who's contagious. He gulped some Heineken.

"You ever try Heineken, Ralph?"

"No."

"You should."

Ralph nodded.

"So the loan. Do you think—?"

"Oh, yeah. The loan. Well, I don't know. I mean, the way I look at it is if I give you a loan, then everyone's going to want one. The next thing I know, Donny's going to have his hand out."

Ralph's head dropped toward the bar slightly.

"It's not like my hand's out," he said.

"But it is. Kind of."

"We don't have to tell anybody."

"People will figure it out once they see you driving a new truck."

"I'll tell them I got a loan from the bank."

"Ralph, everyone knows your credit's shot. That's why you're asking me, isn't it?"

Ralph's head dropped a little more.

"Forget it," he said. "Forget I asked."

"Believe me, Ralph, it's better this way. Friends shouldn't be beholden to each other. That's what kills friendships." Andrew gave Ralph a pat on the back, then slid off his stool.

"I have to get going, Ralph. Peter Beard's giving a party at his place tonight." He stood and turned to Katie. "Wednesday night, Katie."

"Sounds fine."

Andrew left and Katie came over to Ralph. She'd heard most of the loan conversation.

"Who's Peter Beard?" Ralph said.

"I don't know. You want another beer?"

"I better go. Have to fish in the morning."

"It's on me."

"You already bought me one tonight, Katie."

"That's okay. I'll buy you another."

Katie grabbed one of the fresh Buds she'd rotated to the back. She opened it and gave it to Ralph.

CHAPTER 19

Andrew pulled the smoke into his mouth but didn't particularly like the taste of it.

"Enjoying the cigar, Andrew?" Lander Sobel said.

"It's not bad."

Lander laughed smugly.

"I happened to get that one from Castro personally," he said. "It's a Cohiba, the kind he used to smoke himself before he quit."

Jack was there with them at Lander's Bridgehampton mansion. They sat on a semi-circular sofa in front of a giant bay window overlooking the Atlantic. Tonight the moon bathed the water in bluish light, and the ocean's calm, lake-like surface made it seem more like a photograph than real. They were inside despite the large outdoor deck attached to Lander's house. The weather had remained hot since the end of May and many in the Hamptons were experiencing heat fatigue.

"Why don't you give Andrew an art tour?" Jack said, puffing on his own cigar.

"Do you like art, Andrew?" Lander asked.

"Some of it."

"Art's something you'll learn about, along with wine and literature and women."

"I think I know women already."

"Do you?"

"I know what I like."

"One day, Andrew, you're going to wake up and find you want more than just a Barbie doll."

Jack stayed on the sofa smoking his cigar while Lander took Andrew on a tour of his home, pointing out his collection of Picassos, Miros, Pollocks, Warhols and De Koonings.

"These must have cost you a lot," Andrew said, looking closely at each one.

"I like to think of them as an investment, not an expense. Don't blow smoke on them, please."

Lander directed Andrew's attention to a Pollock.

"What do you see?" he said.

"Different color paint splattered around."

"Wrong. Mayhem is what you see. Beautiful mayhem. This painting represents the world as it truly is. Pollock knew exactly what he was doing. Hardly anyone else did at the time. A bloody genius."

He brought Andrew into an oak-paneled room filled with stuffed and mounted animals and a billiard table. Deer and elk and mountain lion heads protruded from all four walls, and a bear skin rug lay on the floor, the head intact, the jaws frozen in a snarl.

"I take it you hunt," Andrew said.

"It's my passion."

"You don't seem the type."

"Cunning and nerve make a good hunter, not machismo. You should know that. You were a fisherman."

Lander sat on a chair upholstered in jaguar skin. He motioned for Andrew to sit in the matching one opposite it, then crossed his legs and tapped his cigar into a standing ashtray mounted on a gazelle leg.

"How do you like it, Andrew?"

"The art?"

"Your new life."

Andrew looked at Lander and noticed his eyes were almost as black as Jack Hawker's.

"Sometimes I can't believe it's actually happening," he said. "I keep thinking I'm going to wake up and be a fisherman again."

"Do you miss it at all?"

"Not really." But Andrew knew he wasn't telling the truth, not entirely. He did miss his old life out on the water, but only in the brief moments when he allowed himself to.

A shallow smile spread across Lander's face.

"You know, the most interesting and challenging hunt I've ever been on was in Africa last year. I'll give you one guess what the quarry was."

"Lion?"

"No. Man."

"I thought that was only in movies."

Lander stood and went over to a small mahogany bar set up in the corner of the room. He poured brandy from a decanter into two large snifters and brought one to Andrew.

"Human quarry," he said, sitting again. "There's nothing quite like it. A secret society in England organizes the trips and only a select few are allowed to go each year. They use black Sudanese slaves as prey. The northern Muslims run the show." Lander drew on his cigar. "No creature in the world is quite as resourceful as man," he said. "Especially one whose life is at stake. Needless to say, most hunters who go to Sudan are unsuccessful."

Andrew looked around the room again, half expecting to see a human head mounted on the wall.

"And you?" he said.

Lander gave him a deadpan look.

"I always get what I'm after." He stood again. "Come with me. I'll show you a piece you might like."

He brought Andrew into another room, this one lighter,

the walls stuccoed like a Mediterranean villa. A fountain consisting of a nude marble nymph with water spurting from her mouth stood at the center of the room. A large painting on the far wall depicted Romans battling fur-clad barbarians. Lander stopped in front of it, and for a minute, he didn't speak as he looked at the bloody scene: soldiers being speared and decapitated, civilians in the process of being eviscerated and raped. A storm raged above the battle, and a helmeted Roman stood unscathed in the midst of everything, pointing the tip of his sword up toward the angry heavens.

"This is my favorite," Lander said. "I see something new every time I look at it."

"Do you look at it often?"

"Almost every day. It calms me. I need calming in my business."

"Dealing art?"

Lander looked at Andrew as if he were an ignorant child.

"Is that all Jack told you about me?"

"Pretty much."

"Well, I do deal art, but that's just a cover, if you will, a front. It's not what I *really* do."

Lander took a quarter from his pocket and flicked it with his thumb. The coin traveled across the room and landed in the fountain at the nymph's feet.

"I'm a venture capitalist, Andrew. I invest my own and other peoples money in various companies and schemes. Some don't pay off. Most do. In the past I've brokered arms deals, usually from the former Soviet bloc to South America. That's how I got into my latest venture. Do you know of a company called AmerGentech?"

Andrew recalled the conversation he'd overheard at Tropper's party.

"I think so."

"I'm surprised. Not many people have."

"They're working on a drug that will allow people to live longer."

Lander tapped some cigar ash into his palm without acknowledging any discomfort.

"Very good, Andrew. Perhaps you should be a stock broker. Anyhow, I've been working closely with AmerGentech, lately. I think this might be my biggest venture yet."

"What are you doing with them?"

"I don't want to bore you with too many details, so I'll explain it in simple terms. You're probably aware that drugs aren't just manufactured out of thin air. They're made from organic substances. This longevity drug AmerGentech is perfecting is no different in that respect." Lander paused to draw on his cigar. "Ten years ago, a scientist named Ethan Whitson discovered a chemical in a rare plant found in the Amazon. This chemical allowed lab mice to live almost fifty percent longer than they normally would. When AmerGentech got wind of it, they made sure Whitson kept his little discovery quiet while he developed it."

"And how are you involved?"

Lander sipped some brandy.

"I make sure AmerGentech has a steady supply of that chemical. It might not sound too complicated or difficult, but it requires the destruction of vast swaths of rain forest, which doesn't make the environmentalists very happy. Naturally, the natives don't seem to mind destroying their own land. They're getting paid. The way I look at it, I'm temporarily alleviating some of their poverty while allowing those who have brighter futures to have longer ones. Meanwhile, I'm making a fair amount from the whole affair."

Andrew searched Lander's face for signs that all of this was another one of his jokes. Lander walked over to the fountain and dropped another coin into it.

"The best ideas are often the simplest ones," he said, speaking to the nymph's feet. "Do you want to be a part of it, Andrew? I can always use investors."

"I'm not sure."

"I can assure you that once this drug hits the market, it's going to dwarf the profits Viagra's been making. Jack's already investing. It would certainly make what you're earning as an actor seem like peanuts."

The whole thing seemed so farfetched to Andrew, like something out of a science fiction movie.

"Do you need an answer right now?" he said.

"Of course not. Let's just enjoy our cigar and brandy."

Lander put his cigar back in his mouth, closed his eyes and sucked in the smoke. Andrew did the same. He still didn't like the taste much.

CHAPTER
20

Katie got in Andrew's SUV and fastened her seatbelt. "Where're we going?" she said.

"You ever been to Sasha and Joe's?"

"I've heard of it. Do they have steak?"

"I'm sure they do."

"I'm really in the mood for steak."

They didn't speak much on the way, and when they got there, Marcus greeted them with a smile. He took Andrew's hand in both of his.

"It's so good to see you, Mr. Kane. You know, this morning. I was walking on the beach and I saw a fishing boat and I thought, 'I wonder if that's Mr. Kane out there.' Then I thought, 'Don't be silly, Marcus. Mr. Kane is a great actor now. He doesn't have to fish anymore.'"

"It could have been a friend of mine's boat," Andrew said, his hand still clutched in Marcus's.

"Of course, Mr. Kane. It must have been a friend of yours. And how is the movie going?"

"Very well, thanks."

Marcus continued to hold Andrew's hand, his smile devolving into the shit-eating variety.

"You know, Mr. Kane, the reason I hold onto your hand is because I want your talent and good fortune to pass to me though our fingers."

"I'd say you already have a lot of good fortune, Marcus. You seem to be the most popular man in the Hamptons. By the way, this is my friend, Katie. Katie, this is Marcus."

"Pleased to meet you, Katie. As the cliché goes, any friend of Mr. Kane's is a friend of mine."

"Now that we're friends, can you get me meals here for free?" Katie said.

Marcus laughed and put his hand on Andrew's shoulder.

"You're lucky to have a friend with such a good sense of humor, Mr. Kane. I've saved a table for you and Katie. Allow me to escort you to it."

Marcus led them to a center table, one of the best and most visible in the house. He pulled the chair out for Katie, then for Andrew. He hovered beside the table after they were seated, his smile beginning to freeze on his face.

"If there is anything at all I can possibly do for you, Mr. Kane, please let me know."

"I will, Marcus. Thanks."

"It's my special pleasure, as always."

Marcus finally left them and returned to his post. Moments later, they heard him saying, "Mr. Kensing, I saw your broadcast last night and I have to say, the way you stay so objective regarding such passionate topics . . ."

"What's his title, Maitre Kiss Ass?" Katie said.

"Something like that."

The attractive young waitress gave them menus. Andrew already knew what he wanted, so he watched Katie reading it. She had let her hair down tonight, and he noticed she'd put on some makeup and mascara, a little more than necessary.

"You look good tonight, Katie."

Katie peered over the top of her menu and seemed surprised by the compliment.

"Who me?"

"Yeah, you."

"You look pretty good yourself."

Katie ordered a salad to start and the hanger steak with garlic mashed potatoes. Andrew ordered the pumpkin raviolis and the Long Island duck special, along with a bottle of Ravenswood pinot noir. Jack had suggested it to him one night and now he ordered it every time. The waitress wrote their orders and departed with the menus, leaving them feeling a little naked with nothing to look at. Katie's smile couldn't completely cover her nervousness.

"So, here we are," she said. "It feels kind of weird."

"Why?"

"We've never really had dinner together, not at a restaurant."

"I thought it would be a nice change," Andrew said, a bit nervous, too. It's just Katie, he told himself. I've known her my whole life. But it occurred to him that perhaps they didn't know each other very well at all anymore, just the parts of themselves that intersected at Moran's.

"I can't even remember the last time I saw you when there hasn't been a bar between us," Katie said.

"Neither can I."

The wine came, a welcome diversion. It was dark and dense and it left thick legs along the inside of their glasses.

"It's good," Katie said, after taking a sip.

"This is one of my favorites."

"So you're a wine expert now."

"I'm trying to expand my tastes."

"In wine or in everything?"

Andrew swirled the wine around his glass and took a sip.

"Life's short," he said. "You should try to experience as much as possible."

"From what I hear, that's exactly what you've been doing."

Katie drank more of the Ravenswood. She might as well be drinking Night Train, Andrew thought. She wouldn't be able to tell the difference.

"We've known each other a long time, haven't we, Katie?"

"Practically our whole lives."

"But it's like we don't really know each other very well. There always seems to be kind of a platonic wall between us."

Katie picked up her fork and inspected it, then put it down and looked back at Andrew.

"You were married for a lot of years, Andrew. Before that, you were the boy living next door with snot running out his nose."

"Well, I'm not married now. And I don't have snot running out of my nose anymore, either."

Katie frowned, as if she was trying to figure out how they'd gotten around to this subject so fast.

"I don't know," she said. "Things never work out in real life."

"I don't believe that."

"I do. Most of the time it's better to let things stay undone. That way you can't be disappointed."

"That's no way to live, Katie." It occurred to Andrew that Jack might have said the same thing.

"It's easy for you to say now," Katie said.

"Why is anything different?"

"Lot's of things are different. You're in a whole other world. Look what happened when you came to the bar the other night. You don't even know how to be friends with Donny and Ralph anymore."

"That's not true."

"Yes it is."

They became silent. Katie inspected her spoon now and Andrew tried to find ways to discredit what she'd just said.

"Katie, I didn't invite you to dinner to argue."

"We're not arguing. I'm just telling you what I think."

The first courses came and the waitress ground pepper over them. The conversation didn't resume when she left. Katie ate her salad quickly and Andrew made an effort to eat slowly, the way the people around them were. Occasionally, he glanced across the table at Katie. She did look good tonight, but what disturbed him was he no longer felt the same yearning for her, the same crush that he always had. Now she was just Katie. Sure, she looked good, but he'd been with better-looking lately—and without all the history and baggage. It made him sad, though, no longer having that feeling, or at least not as much of it.

"How's the salad?" he said.

Katie offered a forkful of red leaf.

"Want some?"

"No, thanks. Want some ravioli?"

"What's in it again?"

"Pumpkin."

"Pumpkin? Never heard of pumpkin ravioli."

"Try some."

Andrew cut one in half and put it on Katie's plate. She ate it.

"Umm. That's good. Pumpkin ravioli. How do you like that?"

The wine was already gone by the time the main courses arrived, but it had done little to ease the discomfort between them. Andrew ordered another bottle, which they finished along with their entrees. Marcus came to the table again.

"Is everything okay, Mr. Kane?"

"Everything's great, Marcus."

"You know, I don't sleep well at night if I know one of my favorite customers was not happy with his meal." He turned to Katie. "Please forgive me, Katie, but what is your last name?"

"Moran."

"Katie Moran. A nice, simple name."

"That's why I like it. It's easy for me to remember."

"I'll remember it, too, Katie Moran."

Marcus left them and Katie blew out her cheeks.

"He's a piece of work," she said.

"Tell me about it."

They ordered coffee and dessert, and while eating it, Katie said, "Are you happier now, Andrew?"

"In what way?" But he knew what she meant.

"Now that you're in this movie and you're making some money."

"It's pretty incredible, isn't it?"

"One in a million chances something like it would happen."

"More like one in twenty million. But you have to take opportunities when they come to you."

"That's what I want to tell Donny and Ralph, but they'd never understand."

Andrew put down his dessert fork and looked at Katie, as if she was the one who would never understand.

"What's not to understand?" he said.

"I guess people don't like being left behind."

"I haven't gone anywhere."

"Maybe that makes it worse, seeing you around, but knowing you're in a different world now." Katie ate some pecan pie and washed it down with coffee. "How are Charlie and Annie doing?"

"They're fine."

"Have you seen them much?"

"No. But I will."

In truth, he hadn't seen them in almost a month. He didn't feel guilty, though, or miss them as much as he usually did. He paid the check and slipped Marcus a twenty-dollar bill on their way out. Marcus dropped it into his jacket pocket and gave Andrew a little bow.

"Thank you for coming, Mr. Kane. And it was my privilege to meet you, Miss Katie Moran."

"You too," Katie said.

The valet brought Andrew's SUV around to the front.

"I don't know how you deal with people like that Marcus guy," Katie said, as soon as they got in. "So phony."

"You get used to it."

"And what's with him and my name?"

"Maybe he's planning to sell it to a gossip columnist."

Andrew turned on the radio and pulled out of the parking lot. "Where to?"

"I should go home."

"How about an after-dinner drink?"

"I'm tired, Andrew. Just drop me off."

Andrew drove the highway back to Montauk and pulled up outside Katie's house on Second House Road. He turned off the engine but kept the radio on. "Harvest Moon" by Neil Young was playing. They sat listening to Neil sing, and when the song ended, Katie said, "Thanks for dinner, Andrew. It was really nice of you."

"Did you like the food?"

"It was great. Can't go wrong with steak."

Andrew planned to kiss her now. He felt sure the rest would flow from there. He moved toward her, a little faster than he intended to. Katie leaned back against the door.

"I don't think we should, Andrew."

Andrew rolled his eyes.

"Christ, Katie. I feel like we're back in high school."

"I thought we were just having dinner."

Andrew returned to his side of the car and rested his hands on the steering wheel.

"Why are you so scared?" he said. "Can't we just have some fun?"

"You've already been having enough fun, from what I hear. You don't need me for that." Katie opened her door, but didn't get out right away. "You know that loan Ralph asked you for?" she said. "The one for a new truck?"

"What about it?"

"You should give it to him. Thanks again for dinner."

She got out and shut the door. She walked up the slate path to the small, ranch-style house she'd grown up in. Andrew watched her unlock the front door and expected her to turn and wave before stepping inside. She didn't.

CHAPTER 21

On his fifth call to her, Penny agreed to his terms. Chad felt good about giving her another chance. He knew that if she hadn't taken it, she would have had to live the rest of her life knowing she should have. He didn't quite have the heart for that.

He'd been calling Penny from the pay phone at Indian Wells Beach, where he'd been sleeping on the dunes since leaving her pool house two weeks ago. He'd stashed his gear and the tapes in the crawl-space beneath the public bathroom there. He didn't like this arrangement much, but knew it would only be temporary, until he concluded the business at hand.

He'd held off on developing Plan B, preferring to renew the offer to Penny every few days. No need to rush, he'd coach himself at night as he lay in the sand, listening to the ocean waves hitting the beach and his windup alarm clock ticking beside his ear. Do it right the first time. He'd made one more copy of the video, just in case, and duct-taped it to the underside of the bathroom floor.

At 1am., Chad arrived at the beachfront house being built about a quarter mile west of Indian Wells. The sky was mostly cloudless and the moon was nearly full, not allowing as much darkness as he had hoped for. He took several minutes to scope out the site. He preferred to make the exchange inside the half-built structure, but knew Penny probably wouldn't feel comfortable going in there with him. He decided they would do it between the house and the dune directly in front of it, hidden from anyone who happened to be walking the beach, as well as anyone driving by on the road.

He stashed the two tapes he'd brought behind a small evergreen on the edge of the lot, then sat on a large rock unearthed by a bulldozer doing cesspool excavation. He looked up at the moon, its edges dulled by the humidity that had continued to thicken as the summer progressed. Don't tell anyone, Mr. Moon, he thought, embarrassed for even thinking such a stupid, childish thought. But he felt happy too, knowing it would be working out after all. Once I have the cash in my pocket, I'm out of here, he thought. Gone. No one will know where I am. And no one will miss me. That made him a little sad, on second thought, not being missed by anyone. But it's the price of freedom, he told himself. Freedom isn't free. He'd heard that in a song once, or maybe in a commercial. He couldn't remember which one.

He picked up a stone and began to pass it back and forth from one hand to the other. He thought of the hundred grand. One hundred thousand dollars. A thousand dollars a hundred times. He thought about how far it would go, what it could buy him. A house here in the Hamptons? Maybe a down payment on one. A Jaguar, perhaps? No, a Rolls Royce. That wouldn't leave much left over, though. He could buy nice clothes and go out to dinner a lot. But he had no one to go to dinner with and he hated sitting alone in restaurants. There was the movie, of course. He had to remind himself that it was the purpose of this to begin with. Yet he couldn't deny that he knew next to nothing about making one. He'd been on sets before, but porn didn't count. And real movies cost a hundred grand a day to make. The low-budget exceptions are exactly that—exceptions.

He considered how long he could live on the money if he decided to play it close to the vest. Five years at the most. A few more if he invested wisely. Then what? Another scheme like this? Suddenly, a hundred grand didn't seem like so much anymore. He wondered if he should demand a hundred and fifty. No. Can't do that. A deal's a deal. I'm a man of honor.

Penny arrived only ten minutes late. She pulled her Range Rover into what would become the driveway, turned off her lights and cut the engine. She got out with a canvas duffel bag slung over her shoulder. Chad stayed seated on the rock and let her search around for him for a bit. Then he called out, "Over here, Penny."

Penny spotted him and came over.

"You're an evil person," she said. "I just thought I'd say that."

"I disagree. But you're entitled to your opinion."

"It's not an opinion. It's a fact."

"Okay. Have it your way." Chad indicated the house with his chin. "Let's go behind there. It's more private."

They started toward the back of the house. The terrain had not yet been graded or leveled, but Penny refused Chad's arm when he offered it to her.

"I think you've made a good decision," Chad said, when they got to the back of the house.

"I don't think I had much of a choice. Do you?"

"That's a good point. Did you bring me the money?"

"No, I brought you a fruit cake."

"A fruit cake?"

"Of course I brought the money, numbskull."

Penny handed Chad the bag. He unzipped it and in the moonlight, he could see the stacks of crisp new twenties. He took one out and riffled the edge with his thumb. The bills created a quick little breeze against his cheek.

"A hundred thousand?" he said.

"A hundred stacks of twenties. Fifty twenties in a stack. You do the math."

"That sounds right." Chad peered down into the bag again. He considered counting the stacks, but knew it would take too long, particularly in the dark. "How did you get all this cash?"

"Let's just say people are willing to do you favors when you travel in my circles. As opposed to yours."

"I plan to be traveling in your circles pretty soon, Penny. Maybe we'll meet at a dinner party over at the Channing place one night."

"I wouldn't hold your breath, trainer boy."

Penny held her hand out to Chad. Chad smiled and shook it.

"No hard feelings, Penny."

"Yes, hard feelings," Penny said, pulling her hand away. "I want the tapes, not your hand."

"Oh, yeah. The tapes."

Chad suddenly felt stupid and clumsy, as if Penny's insults and finally having the money had made him all dopey. He went over to the tree, retrieved the tapes and brought them to her.

"There better not be any more," she said, taking them from him.

"That's all of them," Chad lied.

"Because if another one happens to turn up, I have friends who do other kinds of favors, if you know what I mean."

"Don't worry, Penny. Man of honor. Remember?"

"Don't make me laugh. I'm not in the mood."

They stood facing each other, neither knowing what else to say. Chad smiled. It seemed like the right thing to do.

"We had some fun, didn't we, Penny?"

Penny's hard expression softened a bit.

"We did," she said.

"To tell you the truth, you're the most fun client I ever had."

"Really?"

"Absolutely."

"Good in bed?"

"Very hot."

"That's nice to hear."

Penny smiled too, then she spat in Chad's face, a spray shot that covered his eyes, his nose and his lips. She turned abruptly and walked back to her Range Rover. She gave Chad the finger before getting in and driving off.

Chad wiped Penny's saliva off his face. A small price to pay, he thought. He went back to the rock with the bag of money and sat on it. He opened the bag again and took out a stack of bills. He riffled it and the breeze against his spit-moistened cheek felt good and cooling. He held the stack up to the moon and admired its clean lines. He took off the paper band holding it together and created a fan with the bills, the way he'd seen gamblers do it in the movies. He brought the fan down to his lap and, in the moonlight, he noticed something that stopped his breath, and nearly his heart, too. Except for the top and bottom bills, the rest in the stack consisted of blank paper, not twenties. He checked another stack and found the same thing. He checked several more. No difference. He did a quick calculation and arrived at four thousand dollars in the bag, not a hundred thousand. That fucking bitch!

Chad punched himself in the stomach, then in the chest, then summoned the will to sock himself in the jaw. It hurt like hell, but he felt better for doing it. That should teach you a lesson, dumbass. And what's the lesson? Just when you think you're being smart, you probably being stupid. His jaw began to throb from the blow, but he forced himself to say it aloud.

"Just when you think you're being smart, you're probably being stupid."

He said it again and felt a little better afterward. I'll just have to fix things, won't I? he thought, glad he still had a tape beneath the Indian Wells bathroom and one with a friend in the city. When something breaks, you fix it. That's all. So, he stayed on the rock for the next few hours, considering his options, refining Plan B.

CHAPTER

22

Tom Kendall had taken the night off from B.K.'s, the restaurant he owned on Madison Avenue in Manhattan. He knew from experience that the restaurant business could wear a guy out if he didn't take a night off now and then. It was going to be a quiet evening; he intended to finally finish reading *The Power Broker*, the biography of Robert Moses. But he'd read only a few pages before his bell rang, interrupting him mid-sentence. He put the book down, went to the door, and opened it. He found Karla standing out in the hallway.

"Wally let me up," Karla said. "Can I come in?"

Tom stood aside and let Karla into his apartment. Karla put her handbag on the foyer chair before going into the living room. Tom followed her.

"What are you doing here, Karla?"

"I was in the neighborhood. I thought I'd stop by and say hello. How have you been?"

"I've been fine," Tom said, feeling like a guest in his own apartment. "And you?"

"Not bad. Busy as hell."

Karla sat on the sofa. Tom remained standing.

"Do you have plans for the evening, Tom?"

"I was going to do some reading."

Karla cringed.

"Sounds boring."

"Not everyone can lead such an exciting life."

"That's true." Karla patted the sofa next to her. Tom sat. "We haven't seen each other in a while."

"Maybe that's because you haven't returned any of my calls for the past two months."

Karla dismissed her rudeness with a back-handed wave.

"I said I've been busy, honey."

"Too busy to be courteous?"

Karla rested her hand on Tom's thigh and adopted a more soothing tone.

"It's the column, Tom. It's a beast. It has to be fed constantly."

Tom moved his leg from under her touch.

"I've heard that one before, Karla."

"Well, it's true."

"Then get another profession, if this one drives you crazy."

"What else can I do? I'm made for this job."

"That's too bad."

Karla returned her hand to Tom's thigh.

"Do you hate me, Tom?"

"Why would I hate you?"

"Do you want to see me again?"

"I don't know if I have the energy."

"But you always had plenty of energy."

"I'm talking about emotional."

"Oh, that." Karla shrugged. "Pretend you don't have any emotions. That's what I do."

Tom noticed Karla looking over at his bar, and his hospitality instinct bested his good judgment.

"Would you like a drink, Karla?"

"How about a shot of Jack Daniels and a glass of white zinfindel?"

Tom went to the bar and poured Karla her drinks. He

poured a glass of white zinfindel for himself, as well. He brought them back to the sofa and Karla downed the Jack Daniels in one gulp. She chased it with a large swallow of wine.

"How's business?" she said.

"It's always slower in the summer. It will pick up again in the fall."

"You should open a place in the Hamptons. You can't miss out there, especially if you serve tuna carpaccio. That's what everyone's eating these days. Any celebrities come in lately?"

Tom thought for a few moments.

"Steve Buscemi was in last week."

"Buscemi? Strictly second tier. I'm talking about real stars. They help business, you know."

"I'm aware of that, Karla. So does good food and reasonable prices."

"The mention in my column didn't hurt, did it?"

"No, it didn't. Thank you once again."

Karla took another large swallow of wine. Alcohol always dissolved her inhibitions more quickly and completely than it did most people's. No gradual, easy drunks for her. She leaned closer to Tom and could smell his aftershave.

"Are you seeing anyone, Tom?"

"No one serious."

"You've been waiting for me, haven't you?"

"Come on, Karla."

"I think you have," Karla teased.

"Are you going to start that again?"

Karla placed her hand only inches from his crotch.

"I know what turns you on, Tom."

"Oh?"

"Don't play dumb. It's my powerfulness. I'm a powerful, forceful, liberated woman and that turns you on."

Tom had heard this several times before.

"I knew I shouldn't have given you that Jack Daniels," he said.

"Oh, please. You love this."

Tom laughed.

"You're one of a kind, Karla, thank God."

"You adore me, Tom. Admit it." Karla slid her hand up to his crotch and gave him a squeeze. "See, I knew you adore me."

Tom tried to pull Karla's hand away. She gripped him more tightly.

"You're starting to hurt me, Karla. Men are pretty sensitive down there, in case you didn't know."

"Then don't make me hurt you." Karla maintained her grip. "If you relax, I won't have to."

Karla stood then, and pulled Tom to his feet. With his balls still firmly in hand, she pulled him across the living room and into the bedroom. She let go of him there and quickly unzipped her Donna Karan dress. She kicked off her heels next, and peeled off her black lingerie, nearly tripping as she stepped out of her panties. Tom watched her, becoming increasingly excited despite the pain lingering in his crotch.

"What are you waiting for, Tom?"

Tom undressed too and assumed his usual position with her, on his back. Karla jumped on top of him and grabbed his cock in one swift motion. She aimed it, then dropped onto it and began bouncing up and down, slamming her pubic bone against his.

"I'm fucking you now," she said, through gritted teeth. "I'm fucking you so hard."

Tom reached around and cupped her ass. He arched his back.

"You couldn't resist me, could you?" Karla said, mainly to herself now. "I'm so fucking hot, no man can resist me. I'm a sex machine."

She kept riding, causing Tom to harden even more. She heard his breath begin to come short, quick and shallow, and knew he would climax soon. That was what she wanted. Whoever came first lost.

Then she heard the ringing, a sound she would recognize

anywhere, in any state of mind. She stopped and dismounted.

"What are you doing, Karla?"

"My cell phone. It's in the other room."

"Let it ring."

"It might be important."

"They'll leave a message."

Karla ran from the room to the foyer. She fished her phone from her bag and answered it on the fourth ring. From the bedroom, Tom could hear her speaking, an excited murmur. When Karla returned, she sat on the edge of the bed, but seemed far away now.

"Who was it?" Tom said.

Karla didn't seem to notice him, as if he'd disappeared.

"Could be interesting," she finally answered.

"What?"

"Nothing."

"Let me guess. The column."

Karla stood and gathered her clothes, in a rush now.

"I have to go," she said.

"Where? Can't we finish?"

Karla looked at Tom, as if he were a complete stranger.

"I'm not in the mood anymore. I'll give you a call."

She dressed quickly and left the apartment. On the way out of the building, she asked Wally, the doorman, how his summer had been. She didn't wait for Wally's answer. She just kept walking.

CHAPTER

23

Andrew had no scenes to film, so he took Charlie and Annie to the park across from the Montauk movie theatre. He used to take them there often. Today he had neither the energy nor the imagination to think of anywhere else to go.

The kite he'd bought them resembled a giant bat. He unwrapped it and tied the string to the belly flap. He gave the kite to Annie and the string to Charlie and sent them off across the soccer field with it, Charlie running with the string, Annie holding the kite. But the humidity seemed to be weighing everything down, and the kite kept diving to the ground as soon as she let go of it.

Andrew sat on the bench at the edge of the field and opened the *East Hampton Star*. He hadn't read it in a while, and as he did, he realized how much he'd lost touch with events in the outside world. He ended up skimming most of the front page articles, looking up from time to time to check on the children, who were still having no luck getting the kite airborne. He read more carefully when he got to the entertainment section, searching for anything concerning the movie, particularly mentions of himself.

"Dad, this doesn't work."

Andrew looked up from the paper and found Charlie standing of front of him, with the kite on the ground behind him.

"It works, Charlie. You just have to run a little faster."

"That's what I've been doing. I'm tired now."

"Then sit for a while. Where's Annie?"

"On the monkey bars. Aren't you going to play with us, dad?"

"Let me finish the paper first, Charlie. I don't get much chance to read it anymore."

Charlie kicked at the ground and looked all mopey.

"Mommy says you haven't come to visit us in a long time because you're too busy with the movie," he said, speaking to his feet.

Andrew looked at Charlie again and could see some of his ex-wife in the boy's still-pudgy face.

"A month isn't such a long time," he said. "And don't listen to everything your mother says about me."

He resumed reading, until Charlie tapped his knee.

"Dad, can I come to the movie with you one day?"

"No."

"Why?"

"Because they don't allow kids on the set."

Charlie sat Indian style on the ground in front of him, as if to say, "I'm not going anywhere until you pay more attention to me."

"Are you going to go back to fishing after the movie?" he said.

"I don't think so."

"I hope you do."

"Why?"

"Because then you'll come see us more, like you used to."

Andrew brought the paper down to his lap.

"Charlie, why don't you play with Annie on the monkey bars? I'll be over in a minute."

"Promise?"

"I promise."

Charlie got back to his feet and jogged half-heartedly across the field. He joined Annie on the monkey bars and Andrew watched them climbing, trying to determine exactly what was bothering him. Then he realized that, at the moment, it was boredom. Sitting there on the bench, watching Charlie and Annie on the monkey bars, he couldn't help noticing that kids can be incredibly boring. They were far enough away so he couldn't see their faces very well, and their voices carrying across the field had become generic kid voices. Andrew imagined they could be anyone's, not his own.

He thought back on when both of them were born, the joy he had felt looking at each of them for the first time. He wondered if he would ever feel that kind of joy again, about anything. The children dropped down from the bars and ran back to him. Charlie picked up the kite and gave it another try. Annie climbed into Andrew's lap.

"Daddy, Mary says I have boogers in my nose."

"Who's Mary?"

"She's a girl from the playground."

"You tell Mary everyone has boogers in their nose."

Annie curled into a ball against her father's stomach.

"Daddy, do all little girls have daddies?"

"Of course, they do. You know that."

Annie began to giggle.

"Daddy, do you love Mommy?"

"Why do you ask that?"

"Because you don't live with her anymore."

"Yeah, I love Mommy."

"Are you going to marry her?"

"You ask a lot of questions, don't you?"

"Are you?"

"We already were married, Annie. I can't marry her again."

"Yes, you can," the little girl said, reaching for Andrew's nose and pinching it shut. "I want you to marry Mommy again."

"Well, I don't want to. And I don't think Mommy wants me to, either."

"Why?"

Annie let go of his nose and Andrew took a deep breath.

"Do you want to know why, Annie? I'll tell you why. Because she doesn't love me anymore and I don't love her."

"But you said you did love her."

"I lied."

"Daddy, you told me never to lie."

"Well, sometimes you have to. Now I'm telling the truth."

Charlie managed to get the kite off the ground. He ran across the field with it trailing behind him.

"Look, dad!" he yelled.

"All right, Charlie! Now let some string out!"

Charlie did and the kite stalled and flopped to ground. Annie put her arms around Andrew's neck and nuzzled against him.

"Can we go get ice cream?" she said.

"If you're good."

"Aren't I being good?"

"Yes, you are. We'll go after we stay here a while longer. Why don't you go play with Charlie?"

"I play with Charlie every day. I want to play with you."

"Let me finish the paper first, Annie."

Annie pouted, pushing her lower lip out as far as she could.

"Can't you read the newspaper later when you're not with us?"

"If I read it later, it won't be news anymore. It will be olds."

This quieted Annie for a while. She just sat there watching Charlie struggling to get the kite aloft again. Andrew read about the Yankee game. They had lost the night before. Steinbrenner's going to have to buy some new players in the off-season, he thought. He wondered if he would have been good enough to play for the Yankees had he kept pitching. He checked his watch and figured he could bring the kids back by four, but no earlier. He wondered how to fill the rest of the day with them and considered taking them to a movie. That would kill a couple of hours.

"Daddy?"

"What, Annie?" His sharp tone froze the little girl. He could feel her body tighten.

"Nothing."

Andrew finished the article about the Yankee game and flipped back to the front page. He noticed an article he hadn't seen before. It was about the suicide of a powerful Wall Streeter, an integral player in the leveraged buyouts of the Eighties. He'd made a fortune buying and destroying companies. Friends interviewed said he seemed like the happiest man in the world.

"Do you love me and Charlie, Daddy?"

"Now why do you ask that? Did Mommy put that question in your head?"

Annie shrugged.

"I don't know."

"Well, don't listen to what your mother's been saying about me. Okay?"

Andrew returned to the article, but couldn't see it very well anymore. Tears had begun to cloud his vision. Of course, I love you, Annie, more than anything. He rubbed his eyes clear and continued reading, but only far enough to learn that the dead man had left behind an eighty million dollar estate. Andrew put down the paper and patted Annie's head.

"Come on, peanut. Let's go help Charlie with that kite."

CHAPTER

24

Karla hated having time on her hands, especially such a small amount of it. She had an hour to kill before her meeting at the bank, so she drove slowly through East Hampton, her eyes darting from one side of the street to the other, searching for celebrities. She stopped at the intersection of the Montauk Highway and Newtown Lane and scratched Furball beneath her chin while waiting for the light to change.

"We have an hour, Furball. What do you want to do?"

"Arf!"

"We can't go to the park. It's almost ten o'clock."

"Arf!"

"I already fed you, you little glutton. A half pound of freshly ground filet mignon is plenty. No dog of mine is going to be fat."

"Arf! Arf!"

"You think what? Furball! I'm surprised at you, you little snoop."

The light changed and Karla drove past Newtown Lane. She turned off the highway a mile later and made her way to Lily Pond. She pulled up across the street from Jack Hawker's house, turned off the headlights and the engine, and opened her window.

"Since this was your idea, Furball, I want you to keep your eyes open and your snout shut."

Karla gave Furball another chin scratch, then took the binoculars from the glove compartment. She had bought them in the city, a small but powerful pair that she had tested on the building directly across Fifty-Seventh Street from her apartment. She trained them on Jack's house now.

"I'll bet he's got some innocent young thing in there, Furball," she said, scanning the second floor windows with the binoculars. "Or maybe Simone Tropper for a repeat performance."

Furball let out another bark.

"Quiet, Furball! If we get caught again, you're in big trouble."

Karla aimed the binoculars at the ground floor windows now, moving from right to left until she got to the corner one. And there she saw Jack Hawker, pacing back and forth across the room, moving his mouth and gesturing with his hands.

"I see him, Furball," she whispered. "He's talking to someone. Who do you think? Don't answer. I'll find out. You stay here."

Karla got out of the car and gently pushed the door shut. She walked across the street and took off her heels on the grass. In stocking feet, she tiptoed across the lawn, stopping to hide behind trees and bushes despite the darkness. She had a feeling about this one, reporter's instinct. Scurrying from behind a large oak tree, she tripped over a protruding root. Back on her feet, she noticed her stocking had been torn at the knee and she was bleeding a little. She touched the cut and licked her finger. It tasted good.

When she finally reached the driveway circle, she made a dash for the house, running directly through the tulips, crushing a few of them. She plastered herself against the house and rested a minute, then crouched and inched toward the corner window where she'd seen Jack. Beneath it, she paused for breath again, then slowly straightened up until she could peak inside.

CHAPTER 25

Jack stopped pacing and looked at Lander Sobel, who stood beside the bookcase, smoking a cigar.

"Like I was saying, Lander. You've been doing well with my money. Better than I expected."

Lander nodded, with self-satisfaction.

"Needless to say, I plan to keep up the good work," he said.

"That's what I like to hear."

"And I've been meaning to thank you for giving me the opportunity to help you. It's been a mutually beneficial arrangement."

"Don't bother thanking me, Lander. Not necessary. You know, I was thinking a movie should be made based on you."

"I've never thought of myself as being very dramatic."

"But you are. Very. Of course, you would be the bad guy—a super-villan who claims to be an art dealer but actually deals weapons and munitions, then branches off into destroying the Amazon for fun and profit. It could be a comedy, if we did it the right way."

"I suppose so. I could see you doing the part justice. It would be an honor."

"I was thinking more of Andrew Kane. He's turned out to

be a real thespian. I have to pat myself on the back for that one."

"I think Andrew's developing nicely, really coming around."

A predatory gleam came into Jack's eyes.

"Speaking of developing, have you been developing any new deals for us?"

Lander brightened.

"Just last week I brokered a shipment of AK-47s from the Czech Republic to Sri Lanka. I don't think the little disagreement they've been having there is going to end soon, so I expect they'll need more guns on a continuing basis. We both stand to profit rather handsomely from that one."

"Handsome profits are the best kind. How's your cigar? It's Dominican."

"Excellent. There's nothing like a good cigar." Lander tapped the end of it into an ashtray. "What are you planning to do after the movie is finished, Jack?"

Jack shrugged.

"Who knows? Maybe I'll get a real job. See how the other ninety-nine point nine lives."

"You could always join me as a partner, not just an investor. I think you have a keen mind for business."

Jack walked over to the closed window and looked out of it. He didn't see Karla there, flattened against the house, holding her breath.

"Why risk ruining a good thing?" he said. "I'm difficult to work with, Lander."

"So am I. That's why we might be good together."

Jack turned around.

"I think I'll stick to acting. I'm too lazy to do anything else. What about the AmerGentech thing?"

Lander's brow furrowed a bit.

"It's proceeding. FDA approval shouldn't be a problem. We know several people there who can be persuaded, if you know what I mean. At the risk of sounding optimistic, I think we'll break the bank with this one."

"For me it's the game more than the money. You know that."

"This one might be big game and big money."

"Might be?"

Lander frowned again, more deeply.

"There is one problem. Recently they've been finding that although the drug does considerably extend the human lifespan, it also may cause certain kinds of cancers such as—"

Jack held up his hand.

"No specifics, please, Lander. That shit doesn't interest me. What does is how it's going to get past the FDA if it causes cancer."

"I wouldn't necessarily worry. First of all, they suspect the cancers would take years to appear. And like I said, we know people at the FDA who can be made more than willing to push it through the approval process."

Jack smiled. Lander smiled with him.

"You're one heck of a businessman, Lander."

"I don't know about that. I just don't like to leave any bases uncovered."

Beaming again, Jack stepped away from the window and toward Lander. The deal certainly was promising. He took Lander's face between his hands and kissed him hard on the cheek.

"That's why I love you, Lander, my man. You're thorough, you're smart, and you're modest as all hell." He kissed Lander's other cheek and released his face. "Now, let's go out and get laid. You've earned it."

CHAPTER 26

Still out of breath after sprinting from Jack's window, Karla managed to get her BMW started. Somehow she drove it to the East Hampton Bank parking lot without getting into an accident. Now she sat waiting in the shadow of the oak tree, barely able to contain her excitement.

Jack Hawker is gay, she thought over and over again, trying to assure herself that she'd seen it correctly. He kissed Lander Sobel. I saw it with my own eyes. I'm not crazy. I saw it. JACK HAWKER IS A QUEER! Then she remembered the incident with Simone Tropper in the window and wondered if Marcus had made it up. Wait. Maybe Jack screws women just to keep up appearances. Or maybe he's bisexual. That would be even better. And it would make sense. He swings both ways because he wants everything, the greedy sonofabitch. Perfect! What a column this is going to be. The most macho man in Hollywood is, shall we say, a little light on his toes.

She began to write the column in her head: Okay students, the question of the week is which action/adventure megastar is leading a double life, as it were? Need a hint? His first initial is "J." What do I mean by double life? Let's just say that when it comes to sex, he's a switch hitter. Unsure of your baseball terminology? I'll explain it this way. He hits home runs with both sexes. Enough said for now, students. If you're good and buy lots of magazines, maybe I'll give you more clues and his second initial next month.

OH, MY FUCKING GOD! Karla nearly screamed it out loud. This was going to be the biggest story of the year. No. This was going to be the biggest story of the decade. I'll go back to Jack's house every night, if necessary. I don't want to miss a thing. She turned to Furball.

"You don't believe Mommy Goddess, do you, Furball? You can't accept that your favorite actor in the world is a living a big, fat lie, can you?"

Furball barked, loudly.

Karla head-spanked the dog, then gripped the wheel more tightly. She tried yoga breathing to calm herself. It didn't help. He kissed Lander Sobel, she thought. Not once, but twice. He held his face in his hands and kissed him. Then they left the room. I bet they went upstairs and got right down to business. Karla attempted more yoga breaths. Control. Control. You're Karla Sands. Karla Sands doesn't lose control. Karla Sands is the consummate professional.

She began to feel a little calmer. It's going to go right in the column, she assured herself, *very* thinly disguised. John Meade can take a flying leap out his beloved window. I'll make it into a series, a serial. I'll do some more spying and leak clues each issue. I'll build the suspense until people can't bear it anymore. She considered driving back to the city now, getting to work right away. Hang on. I can't go yet. I have a meeting. Karla checked her face in the mirror. More dirt on the way, she thought, fixing an eyeliner smudge. When you're on a roll, you have to keep it coming. That's what a reporter of my caliber does.

The passenger door opened minutes later. Karla jumped a little and Furball began to bark again.

"Are you Karla Sands?"

"I am."

"I'm Chad. We spoke on the phone."

"Oh, yes. Chad. I didn't see your car."

"I walked."

"Hop in."

Karla lifted the barking terrier into the back seat and Chad got in.

"Nice to meet you, Mrs. Sands," he said, extending his hand to Karla.

"It's Ms. Sands," Karla said, shaking it. "How did you find me?"

"I saw your column in *Boulevard*. I called the office and they give me your cell number."

"That's good. I like it when readers get involved. What do you have for me?"

"Do you know Penny Baskin?"

"Sure, I do. She's Francis Baskin's wife. What's your connection to her?"

"I'm her personal trainer. I used to be, anyway."

"I'm listening."

"You don't have to listen. Take a look instead."

Chad unzipped his gym bag and took the video camera from it. He handed it to Karla and pressed the "Play" button. The camera's tiny LCD screen lighted up.

Karla looked down at the screen and watched the entire tape. Chad took the camera back from her when it ended.

"What do you think, Ms. Sands?"

"You can call me Karla, if you want, Chad."

"Okay, Karla."

"I think you and I can do some business, if that's what you're here for."

"That's exactly what I'm here for."

Karla quickly scanned the empty parking lot and lowered her voice to just above a whisper.

"Has anyone else seen this tape?"

"No."

"I want an exclusive, then, which means no one else sees it."

"That will cost you."

"You're quite the businessman for a personal trainer."

Chad suppressed a smile.

"I do what I have to do," he said.

"I can see that. You and I should consider working together more."

"What do you have in mind?"

Karla eyed Chad's camera and imagined all the celebrities it could be used to spy on.

"I'm sure you have other rich, high profile clients," she said.

"I'm getting out of personal training."

"What do you intend to do?"

"I'm not sure. I might make a movie."

Karla laughed.

"Sorry. I didn't mean to laugh." She put her hand on Chad's thigh and deepened her voice to seductive. "Forget about movies for now, Chad. Let's discuss what we can do for each other."

"I'm going to need money if you want the tape."

Karla moved her hand up his thigh.

"You surprised me, Chad."

"How?"

"You're a lot sexier than I expected you to be."

"Thanks. You're a nice looking lady, too."

"Lady? I'm not a woman?"

"That's what I meant."

"I thought so. What price were you looking for?"

"A hundred and fifty grand."

Karla raised her eyebrows.

"That's steep."

"If it's too much for you, I can go somewhere else with it."

"No, no, no. Don't do that."

Karla dug her fingers into Chad's leg, buying herself time. The kid has a nice body, she thought, but he certainly doesn't have any brains. He would have gone to television with the tape first, if he did. Now that I've seen it, I don't need it anymore. But I can't let him show it to anyone else. How can I accomplish this without paying him anything? That's the question.

"Do you live around here, Chad?"

"I'm from the city."

"Really? You seem too sweet to be a New Yorker."

"I'm from the Midwest originally. Minnesota."

"Cold there. Nice people, though, from what I hear."

"Yeah, real nice. So, are you going to buy the tape? I haven't shown it to anyone else yet."

"Promise?"

"I'm a man of honor."

"I trust you, Chad. How could I not trust someone from Minnesota?"

Karla thought of her last meeting here, with Marcus, that slimy bastard. But he did give her an idea, a possible solution. Men want sex, don't they? All of them do. This one is definitely no exception. I'll take him down to the beach and make him an offer he can't refuse. I'll also ask him where he bought his little video camera. One of them would be perfect for documenting Jack Hawker's escapades.

"Do you want to go for a ride somewhere, Chad? It's a nice night out."

"Sure."

"How about Indian Wells Beach?"

"That sounds fine."

Karla started the car. This is the greatest night of my life, she thought, driving across the parking lot toward the Montauk Highway. No doubt about it. I have two huge new stories, as dirty as they come. And they're all mine. The *News* and the *Post* won't have anything on me this month. Now all I have to do is pleasure this low-life a bit. It shouldn't be too bad. At least he has a nice body.

PART FIVE
LABOR DAY WEEKEND

CHAPTER 27

Jack showed up at Andrew's house around ten-thirty that night. He hadn't called ahead and he entered without knocking. He went into Andrew's bedroom, where Andrew lay trying to sleep.

"I can't believe you're still living here," Jack said, standing beside Andrew's bed. "You drive a brand new Mercedes SUV and you're living in a shotgun shack. Doesn't make sense."

Andrew sat up and rubbed his eyes. He'd gone to bed early for the first time in weeks.

"I grew up here," he said. "It's about the only thing I still have from the old days."

"Well, get up. We're going for a ride."

Andrew didn't feel like going for a ride, but knew Jack well enough to know he wouldn't take no for an answer. He got out of bed and dressed. They took Jack's Porsche and headed west on the old section of highway that brought them to the Napeague flat. Not many cars were on the flat and the night was unusually clear, the stars shining brightly, the moon white and three-dimensional. Andrew caught glimpses of the water through breaks in the dunes, the moonlight shining down on it. Jack began to hum the same eerie tune he had hummed on the beach after the Tropper party. Then he stopped humming and looked at Andrew.

"Tell me, Andrew, how do you like it?"

"Your humming?"

"Being an actor."

"It's okay."

"Okay? You're going to be a star. You're already getting more ass than a toilet seat. You got a little money, too, and it's just okay?"

"It's been great. What can I say?"

"That's more like it."

Jack turned on the radio and tuned it to WEMH. The news came on and the top story was the Donahue family's plea for Seth's killer to turn himself in. Jack turned off the radio.

"Old Seth's getting more press now than he did when he was alive," he said.

"I wonder what happened to him."

"His head got cut off. That's what happened to him."

Andrew didn't want to discuss it any further. He still felt a bit guilty for taking Seth's role.

"Poor guy," he said.

"Don't worry. He's not suffering anymore. Who knows? Maybe he's having more fun now."

"Is that what it's all about, having fun?"

"What's more important than that?"

Jack accelerated past two cars at once, sneaking back into his lane just in front of an oncoming 18-wheeler.

"Jesus, Jack! You trying to kill us?"

"Jack Hawker is always in complete control," Jack said, looking at Andrew, not at the road. "You ever seen me get killed in any of my movies? Have you?"

Jack returned his eyes to the road and Andrew looked out at the water, wishing he was on *Bessie* right now.

"You know, you're a real notch on my belt, Andrew."

"Thanks . . . I guess."

"No, really. You're my Eliza Doolittle. It's like I found a diamond in the rough and polished it."

"Is that how you see me?"

Jack reached over and pinched Andrew's chin.

"You could stand a little more polishing, don't get me wrong."

He pulled up behind a red pickup truck driving the speed limit. Andrew immediately recognized it to be Ralph's. He wondered where Ralph was going.

"This is why I hate driving out here," Jack said.

"It's a friend of mine."

"One of the Moran's losers?"

"Depends on your definition of loser," Andrew said, restraining the urge to sock Jack in the jaw.

Jack pulled into the oncoming lane and Andrew didn't look at Ralph as they passed him. But he felt like telling Jack to stop. He felt like waving Ralph over and telling him he'd buy him that new truck. Whatever kind you want, Ralph. You wouldn't have to pay me back.

"Fucking bonackers drive about as fast as they think," Jack said. "Oops. Sorry, Andrew. I forgot. You used to be a bonacker."

"I still am."

Jack finally slowed coming into Amagansett. They stopped for a drink at Atlantic, packed with young New York women dressed to the nines on this Labor Day weekend. Jack ordered a whiskey and Andrew ordered a beer. They drank and didn't talk much. Mostly, they watched the women, who watched them back but were too shy to approach without being beckoned.

"I'm not in the mood for it tonight," Jack said.

"That's a first since I've known you."

"Most of them are bitches, in case you hadn't noticed."

"What about Gwendolyn?"

Jack let out a quick laugh.

"Gwendolyn's the evilest of them all. At least she's got a sense of humor."

They finished their drinks and left the bar. Jack drove west through Amagansett, past the crowded bars there. The village ended after only a few blocks, and the highway continued past some nurseries and the American Legion Hall and Bob's General Store. They passed some more nurseries after the Abraham's Path intersection, then a cluster of summer cabins, then La Chiquita Latina, which served rice and beans to the Hispanic landscapers who worked the estates all along the East End.

"You hear about Karla Sands?" Jack said, pulling up behind an old Dodge.

"No."

"Bitch finally got canned from *Boulevard Magazine*. She tried to write about a videotape she saw of Francis's wife getting it on with a guy in a leather mask. Her editor told her to take a hike." Jack smiled. "I guess her chickens finally came home to roost."

"How did you find out?"

"It's my job to keep tabs on those who keep tabs on me, Andy boy. The asshole who made the tape got arrested for extortion. Just goes to show that crime doesn't pay." Jack pulled up closer to the Dodge. "Motherfucker," he grumbled, nosing the Porsche out of its lane.

The oncoming traffic forced him back in.

"What's the rush, Jack?"

"I'm not rushing. Everyone else is slow."

Jack nosed the Porsche out again. Still no break in the oncoming traffic. But this time, he made his move, straddling the line.

"Don't worry," he said. "I did this in *The Kill Squad*. No stunt man."

He accelerated until he'd pulled up beside the Dodge, leaving only inches between the two vehicles. Andrew gripped his armrest and kept quiet. He knew saying anything now would only increase the danger. Oncoming cars sounded their horns and flashed their lights as they whizzed by, sandwiching the Porsche between them and the Dodge.

A Jitney bus approached, too wide to pass without clipping the Porsche. It too sounded its horn and flashed its lights. Andrew gripped the armrest more tightly as it came closer. He thought of Charlie and Annie, of never seeing them again. The bus driver leaned on his horn and Andrew instinctively ducked as it bore down on them.

Jack jerked the wheel at the last moment, banging his Porsche against the Dodge, forcing it off the road. He swerved into the right lane just before the bus passed. His head still down, Andrew heard the Dodge's tires squealing against the tarmac. He straightened up and looked back in time to see it skidding into a telephone pole. He saw its windshield shatter and spray, and heard the sickening sound of metal folding around wood. Jack stepped on the gas.

"Aren't you going to stop, Jack? He's probably hurt."

Jack didn't answer at first. He kept his eyes fixed on the road ahead of him, as if nothing had happened. Then he said, "If he's hurt, there's nothing we can do about it now."

"We have to call the police."

"Someone else will. Everyone out here has a cell phone. Let's go to the Red Monkey and get a margarita."

"We have to go back. That guy might be dead."

"Sorry Andrew, no can do. Why don't we get something to eat at Sasha and Joe's? We'll go over tomorrow's scene. It's going to be a good one."

Andrew felt his throat closing up on him.

"Go to the beach," he said. "Drive me to the beach and leave me there. Do you understand?"

Jack turned and Andrew could feel his stare boring into him.

"You shouldn't take life so seriously, Andrew. It's going to be over before you know it."

"Just take me to the beach."

"Have it your way."

Jack turned off the highway and headed south toward the water. He pulled into the beach parking lot and Andrew got out of the car. He closed the door before Jack could say anything, and walked to the edge of the sand. He stood there peering into the darkness, and didn't turn around until he heard Jack pulling away.

CHAPTER 28

Jack's taillights disappeared into the night, and Andrew started down the beach. He planned to walk all the way home, but the soft sand quickly sapped his energy. So he stopped and sat in the sea grass at the base of a dune and watched the waves breaking in the dark. He saw the Dodge running off the road with each white burst of foam. He saw it smashing into the telephone pole and the windshield spraying like drops of water. Over and over again, he saw it.

He sat there the entire night, dozing from time to time, but mostly wide awake. He watched the sky lighten in the morning, and the sun rise. He had been awake for almost every sunrise since becoming a fisherman, but had only watched it like this that one time with Katie. He wished she were here now, watching it with him again.

He thought back over the last few months. They seemed like an eternity. Strangely, he could only recall certain details and disconnected scenes, but no continuum of events or people except for Jack—whom he considered a presence more than a person. He wrote a crude balance sheet in his head, weighing what he had gained against what he had lost. Sitting there against the dune, it seemed to him that he'd lost just about everything worth having.

He stood and walked down to the water, rough today, the waves coming in at varying angles. He had heard radio reports of a storm approaching from the south. He took off his shoes, then stripped off his clothes and walked into the water. The waves broke against his stomach, each one knocking him back a step or two. He dove into the base of one and grabbed onto the bottom. The water surged over him, pushing him back toward the beach. He held on until it passed, then stood and dove into the next, then the one after that.

The waves came quickly, with little pause or break between them. Normally, Andrew would have retreated, or not ventured in at all. But he felt no fear this morning, only the desire to be washed clean. A large wave curled toward him. Andrew didn't dive under this one. He stood firm and squared himself. The wave smashed into him, knocking him off his feet and pulling him under. He regained his footing and moved back out to face the next one.

He let them knock him down again and again, until he barely had the strength to stand anymore. Then he made his way back onto the beach, where he lay on his shirt and stared up at the sky that had lightened to a blue made pastel by the fresh humidity hanging beneath it. He heard the waves crashing and felt each one vibrating the beach ever so slightly. This rhythm soothed him into sleep.

The sun had risen to a forty-five degree angle by the time he woke again. He sat up and watched a few strollers playing tag with the wave tongues. A dog chased after a Frisbee and a young couple walked by, hand in hand. Andrew wished he was the man holding the woman's hand. He wished he could take her home and make love to her, then sleep next to her and wake in the afternoon to eat a plate of scrambled eggs in bed. He imagined cuddling with her and kissing her all over, not just on her lips. That woman became Katie in his imagination, and it seemed so right, him being that man, Katie being the woman with him.

He stood and brushed the sand off him. And instead of heading east to Montauk, he turned west toward East Hampton. He began to walk, feeling stronger after having slept. The salty air felt good flowing into his lungs, and his head seemed clearer than it had been in a long time. He wondered what Charlie and Annie were doing at this exact moment, and decided he would fly that kite with them again, really get it up there. He would also buy them ice cream and take them fishing in Fort Pond and give them a thousand hugs and kisses.

He walked for nearly an hour, keeping his eyes on the point of beach ahead, obscured by the mounting humidity and a cloud of ocean spray. He moved toward the point with a robotic sense of purpose and began to feel good for the first time that he could remember, as if a weight had fallen off his back and his chest and his head.

He stopped when he reached Jack's house, its glass front watching the ocean like a giant eye. He stood before it, then spotted a path over the dunes and walked it to the house. He went to the door, rang the bell and waited. Jack opened the door a minute later, wearing a silk bathrobe, his hair tousled from being in bed.

"Andy boy. You came to apologize for being so mean to me last night."

"I didn't come to apologize for anything."

"You're still mad about what I did?"

"You might have killed somebody."

A woman in a matching robe came up behind Jack. She wrapped her arms around his waist and propped her chin on his shoulder. Andrew recognized her as the waitress from Sasha and Joe's.

"Andrew, this is Betsy. Betsy, this is Andrew."

"Hi, Betsy. We've met before."

Betsy smiled, but her eyes looked clouded, as if she'd been doing drugs or drinking.

"Betsy, why don't you wait for me in the bedroom?" Jack

said. "I'll take you to the moon again in a minute."

Betsy unwrapped her arms from around Jack and headed back to the bedroom.

"Sometimes the quiet ones are best in the sack," Jack said, with a wink.

"So, you run a man into a telephone pole, then go to Sasha and Joe's afterward."

"A man has to eat. Now what the fuck are you doing here? I'm busy, if you hadn't noticed."

Andrew looked Jack in the eye.

"I want out of the movie."

Jack laughed.

"You really are something, Andrew."

"I've had enough."

"Enough of what?"

"Of this. Of everything."

"That's what I like about you, Andrew. You're so damned articulate."

"You know what I'm talking about."

Jack's smile disappeared.

"Yeah, I do know what you're talking about. Now you should know what I'm talking about, too. You signed a contract. And we're well into shooting. You can't pull out now and leave us high and dry."

"Sure I can. I just won't show up on set."

Jack stepped closer and his morning breath wafted into Andrew's face.

"If you're trying to strong-arm me for more money, I wouldn't if I were you."

"Money's got nothing to do with it."

"What is it, then? Big Jack Hawker play too rough for you?"

Jack was right. He did play too rough. But Andrew no longer cared what Jack thought of him.

"Something like that," he said.

Jack looked over Andrew's shoulder, as if he'd spotted

something interesting out on the water.

"You may not believe this," he said. "But I've been bored shitless lately. Maybe that's why I've been acting out, as it were." His gaze returned to Andrew. "Tell you what. I'll let you out of the film. What do I care? We'll just have some script doctors write you out of the ending, have you drink yourself to death or something."

"You're going to let me out, just like that?"

Jack held out his hands in a stop gesture.

"I wouldn't thank me yet if I was you. You're going to have to win your release. If you do, you can go back to chasing sardines and bar maids."

"I'm not sure I follow."

Jack stepped aside and motioned Andrew into his house.

"Come on in, sailor. We'll have some eggs and talk about it."

CHAPTER

29

The rules were simple. Whoever caught the biggest shark by sundown, won. It didn't matter what kind of shark, as long as it was caught using a rod and reel, bait and hook. Jack had called a halt to the shooting so they could do it the following day. Andrew went home and slept. He woke early the next morning and was surprised to actually find Jack waiting for him at the Sag Harbor Yacht Club.

"Didn't think I would show, did you?" Jack said.

"I had my doubts."

Jack had given *Diablo*'s crew the day off, so he drove the boat himself. He took her out of the harbor and guided her east through Gardiners Bay, the Peconic, then past Gardiners Island and Montauk Point into open water. A steady wind blew from the south, and the sky looked dark and heavily clouded. *Diablo* bounced through the combination of chop and swells. Andrew sat up by the bow, fully experiencing her motion.

"I brought some refreshments," Jack called to him from the bridge, holding up a bottle of Jamesons.

He drove *Diablo* fast and cut her engines ten miles past the Point, letting her drift with the current. He came down to the lower stern deck, where Andrew sat scanning the water for signs of life. To be completely fair, they had decided to use the exact same gear: heavy fiberglass rods, Shimano reels with quadrant drag brakes, eighty pound monofilament line, fifteen foot #10 wire leaders, snap swivels, and triple strength martin hooks. They each prepared their tackle and Jack put on a gimbal belt fitted with a bucket for the butt of his rod. He gave one to Andrew.

"We're going to fight them standing up," he said. "None of that pussy chair shit."

"What about gaffing and roping?"

"If you bring one to the side of the boat, the other guy has to grab the leader and gaff the tail. He can't slack it, either."

"Fair enough."

Jack went over to the fish hold and brought out a large bucket of ground up menhaden fish. He brought out another bucket, a smaller one filled with whole bunker. They both baited their hooks with a bunker, inserting the point into the throat and pushing it out the stomach. Next, Jack brought the chum bucket to the gunwale and began to ladle the menhaden into the water. He had created a nice chum line before long, extending out several hundred feet from the stern. Then they set their drag brakes and dropped their lines in. For the next hour they took turns ladling chum, but neither of them saw or caught anything.

"You can't beat me, Andrew," Jack said, after a long silence.

"What makes you say that?"

"Because I'm Jack Hawker. You ever seen me lose?"

They focused on fishing and Jack soon caught a ten pound mackerel, which he tossed into the fish hold. Andrew pulled in his line and put a fresh bunker on the hook.

"I want to remind you how generous I'm being," Jack said. "This is a one-way bet, if you hadn't noticed. If I win, I don't gain anything I don't already have."

"This was your idea, not mine."

The wind had picked up and the chop splashing against *Diablo* began to throw up a spray.

"A storm's moving up the coast," Andrew said.

"You scared?"

"Nothing scares me anymore."

"*Nothing scares me anymore*," Jack mimicked. "Captain Courageous here."

Jack opened the bottle of Jamesons and drank some. He offered it to Andrew, who refused. Andrew ladled some more chum into the water. The thing was to keep the chum line unbroken, lead the sharks right to the boat. He scanned the water for small fish jumping, for birds diving after them—any indication that sharks might be nearby. Jack caught a bluefish, about the twice the size of the mackerel. He took it off the hook and held it up to Andrew before throwing it into the hold.

"Too bad we're not going for the small fries," he said. "I seem to be better at catching them than you are, Fisherman."

"It's mostly luck, you know."

"That's what all losers say."

The hours passed slowly and, as the storm approached, the swells increased in size and frequency. Andrew began to feel a little seasick for the first time that he could remember. He pulled in his line again and rebaited his hook.

"You and I have a fight scene coming up in the movie," Jack said. "The big, climactic fight scene. Fitting, isn't it?"

"Sounds exciting," Andrew said. "You have to win this first, though."

"Oh, I will. You know, I was thinking earlier that I should have signed you to a multi-film contract. You would have signed your own death warrant that night at the party. Not that you're a good actor or anything. Anyone can play themself." Jack drank some more Jamesons and a devious twinkle came into his eyes. "You see, if I had signed you on for more films, I could have done anything I wanted with you. Instead of grooming you into a successful actor, I could have just as easily destroyed you, put you in one embarrassingly bad movie after another. Remember Cory Haim? Scott Biao? How about Shaun Cassidy? I could have modeled you on anyone of those nitwits."

"You're a real sweetheart, Jack."

"So they say. Yeah, I'd have you languish in one clunker after another, just for the fun of it. You'd become the butt of every Hollywood joke. Letterman and Leno would have a field day with you. Ah, America. You got to love it. We tear down and humiliate our heroes like no other country in the world."

Andrew had stopped listening. He knew it wouldn't help him catch anything. The heavy clouds were nearly upon them by now, and it made him a little nervous. Then a pack of blue sharks appeared, five or six of them. Jack jigged his line and popped his bait out of the water, like a live fish jumping.

"Come to daddy, fuckers," he said. "It's snack time."

The sharks began to dart through the chum, gulping it down. They concentrated on the chum for a while, until finally the biggest one struck Jack's bait. Jack waited until it had swallowed the hook before jerking his rod back and setting the barb deep it its mouth. He released his brake and loosened the drag as the shark made its run, bolting straight out from the starboard side, peeling line off the reel at a furious rate.

"Got myself a live one!" Jack hollered. "I'm going to need you as my wingman, Andrew!"

Andrew pulled his line from the water. Since they needed each other to grab the leader and gaff the tail, both couldn't catch a shark at the same time; it was part of the rules. Jack tightened his drag when the shark came to the end of its first run. He pulled back hard on his rod and began to crank in the slack he'd created. The shark made several more runs, and Jack had to loosen his drag each time or risk a snapped line. The shark moved around the boat, forcing Jack to follow it, keeping his line clear of obstructions. Once, the shark torpedoed under the boat, and Jack dipped the tip of his rod into the water to keep the line from being cut on barnacles attached to the hull. He kept the pressure on the fish, though, pulling back and reeling in slack. Soon he was drenched in sweat and his arm muscles were bulging. But he didn't seem to be tiring at all. The shark did, though, each of his runs becoming shorter and less vigorous. Jack had regained most of his line within twenty minutes.

"Get ready, Andy boy!" he yelled.

He pumped the reel some more and brought the shark to the side of the boat. Andrew leaned over the gunwale and grabbed onto the leader when it broke the surface. The shark thrashed and rolled and its jaws snapped open and shut, trying to bite through the leader—and Andrew's arm. Andrew used all of his strength to pull the shark's head and half its body out of the water. It was a big fish, over ten feet long. Jack dropped his rod and grabbed the flying gaff, which had a nylon rope attached to it. He raised it up and sank it into the shark's back, just behind its dorsal fin. He wound the gaff rope around a deck bitt while Andrew grabbed the straight gaff and planted it into the shark's violently thrashing tail. He pulled hard, lifting the tail out of the water, taking away most of its leverage. Jack came behind Andrew and secured a thicker rope to the tail, pulling its sliding loop tight just behind the lobes. He secured that rope to another bitt.

"We'll be eating shark steaks tonight, Andy boy!"

With the shark under control now, they winched it up onto the ginpole and secured a belly rope around its stomach to keep it from thrashing anymore.

They both sat to rest.

"It's at least ten feet long," Jack said, admiring the shark he'd just caught. "Damned big for a blue."

"We'll do it by weight, not length."

"We didn't specify that, did we? I'll have to consult my lawyer." Jack drank some Jamesons. "All right. What the hell? We'll do it by weight."

The wind had picked up and a light rain began to fall. In normal circumstances, Andrew would have turned around and headed back to the docks. He rested a few more minutes, then ladled more chum into the water. He and Jack dropped their lines in again, and more blue sharks soon appeared. But these seemed content to feast on the chum and leave the bait alone, perhaps spooked by what had happened to their friend. They followed *Diablo* for several miles before suddenly disappearing. Andrew knew it had to be for a reason, often the presence of a larger, fiercer type of shark. He also knew the larger ones usually stayed below the surface until they decided to strike. He peered down into the slate-colored water, but didn't see anything until a lone dorsal, a huge blue-gray triangle, broke the surface several yards off port. Slowly it circled the boat, ignoring the chum.

"That's a mako," Jack said, softly, staring at it with a hungry look in his eyes.

"I think you're right."

"Look at the size of that fin. Probably eight hundred pounds or more."

They watched the shark move closer to the boat, as if stalking it. Jack poured some whiskey into his mouth, never taking his eyes off the shark.

"That one's got my name on it," he said.

"Maybe it has its name on you."

"I wouldn't bet on it."

They didn't speak anymore, both mesmerized by the huge mako trolling beside them, neither thinking about the movie or the purpose of the contest anymore. Now, it was only about catching that shark, testing themselves against it and against each other. The fish turned toward *Diablo* and seemed ready to ram her hull, but dove beneath it at the last moment. It reemerged on the other side and began to circle again, still ignoring the chum and bait.

"It doesn't seem hungry," Andrew said.

"Not for fish, anyway."

"I'd say whoever lands this one probably wins."

"That's a fair assumption," Jack said.

The shark still seemed more interested in the boat. It darted toward it again, turning at the last moment and swimming away. Andrew was surprised to see Jack put down his rod, resting it against the gunwale. He swigged more whiskey, then went back toward the fish hold behind them. Intent on catching the shark, Andrew kept his eyes on the water, forgetting about Jack and what he was doing. He jigged his line a couple of times, trying to attract the shark. Then came the blow to the back of his head. It stunned him more than hurt. He tried to keep his balance, but his legs crumpled, their muscles suddenly useless. He hit the deck hard and the light began to fade as he slipped into a black, soundless hole.

CHAPTER 30

Andrew came to with his head on fire and his vision blurred. He could feel the cool, wet deck against his cheek and warm blood dripping down the back of his neck. He didn't know where he was at first and hoped he had merely fallen into another nightmare. Then he felt a throbbing where the blow had landed and knew this was real. He reached back and touched the wound, the pain more intense than any he'd ever experienced. He brought his fingers to his face and could see the blood on them. As his vision cleared, he saw Jack standing at the gunwale, his rod in one hand, the flying gaff in the other.

"Feeling a little headachy, Andrew?" he said. "I think there's some aspirin somewhere on the boat."

Andrew tried to get to his feet, but couldn't move his legs. He tried to speak, but couldn't do that, either. He felt the back of his head again, wondering how badly the blow had damaged him.

Jack began to chuckle.

"Okay, Andrew, I'll tell you why I hit you on the head with the back of this nifty little flying gaff. I don't like to lose. That's why. I never have and I don't intend to start now."

Jack hooked the gaff on the gunwale and jigged his line.

"Who loves you, Mr. Shark?" he said, into the water. "Who loves you?"

He looked at Andrew again.

"You seem kind of beat, Andy boy. Pun intended, of course. Don't worry about trying to move or speak. You won't be able to for a while, thanks to the stunt fighter who taught me just where to hit a guy." He looked back at the shark. "I know what you want, Mr. Big Shark Guy. You want some nice, fresh bluefish, don't you?"

He fitted the butt of his rod into a fighting chair gimbal, then went over to a tool locker built into the deck. He flipped the latch, opened the locker, and took a large military machete from it. Andrew watched him go over to the fish hold next, and pull out the bluefish he'd caught. He placed the still live fish on the deck, crouched beside it and began hacking it to pieces with the machete, a determined, almost maniacal look on his face.

A military machete. At that moment, Andrew knew. Jack had killed Seth Donahue, with that very machete. His heart began to race and pound. He had no idea what to do next.

Jack suddenly looked up from the butchered fish. His eyes met with Andrew's, then flicked down to the machete, covered with fish blood. A quick little laugh escaped his lips. He stood and walked over to Andrew, still holding the weapon.

"You think I killed Seth Donahue, don't you?" he said, standing over him. "I can see that's what you're thinking."

Andrew tried to speak, but still couldn't. He felt dizzy as more blood dripped from his wound and down the back of his neck.

"And I bet detective Andrew Kane thinks I used this machete to do it."

Jack began to chuckle again, but his eyes remained hard and cold.

"You're good, Andrew," he said. "But then it doesn't take a genius to put two and two together. Okay, I killed him. End of mystery. I took him fishing on old *Diablo* here and I lopped his noggin off with this handy machete." Jack moved closer to Andrew and tightened his grip on the weapon. "But why? Andrew Kane probably wants to know why I killed Seth Donahue. To tell you the truth, Andy boy, I don't really know for sure. I just did it. It seemed like the thing to do at the time."

Andrew tried to stand, but still couldn't move his legs. His heart was pounding in his temples and his throat had gone bone dry. He struggled to manufacture enough saliva to swallow and he kept his eyes on Jack, sure Jack would kill him now, as well. Then Jack's eyes softened a bit.

"You know how many people I've killed in my movies, Andrew? Four hundred and fifty-six. But until a few months ago, I'd never actually killed anyone for real. Not one god-damned person. For me, killing Seth was the ultimate method acting. Now I can bring some reality to my movies." Jack shook his head, as though with remorse. "It didn't have to be Seth, but he was there and I was a little drunk. Okay, a lot drunk, but what does it matter?"

He tapped the machete blade against his leg and began turning it in his hand. Andrew imagined what it was going to feel like, the blade cutting through his flesh.

"It's funny how you're the one who found him, isn't it?" Jack said. "I kind of figured it was one of you fisher guys. When I saw you there at Moran's, I pretty much knew it was you."

"You're crazy," Andrew managed to whisper through parched throat and lips.

Jack acted surprised and a little hurt. He cupped his bloody hand behind his ear.

"What was that? Andrew Kane thinks I'm crazy? Well, maybe I am. Then again, maybe I'm not. Who's to say for sure?" He sat beside Andrew and fell into a deep think. "But I do have a little dilemma," he said, snapping out of it. "On the one hand, I don't really need you for the movie. Script doctors. Remember? On the other hand, another body on my resumé might not be the wisest thing. So, what am I to do now? Maybe I'll use this machete to turn you into chum. I'll tell Pistol Pete, your Sheriff buddy, that the shark pulled you overboard and ate you for lunch before I could capture it. I'll get all sad and teary when I tell him how I tried to save you and all." Jack glanced at the water, then back at Andrew. "I'm not boring you with my rambling, am I?"

Just then, the mako took Jack's bait, hitting it hard, nearly pulling the rod overboard before he could grab it, release the drag brake, and insert the butt into his gimbal belt. The mako ran nearly twice as fast as the blue shark had, but it stopped after only fifty yards, turned and headed back toward the boat. Andrew watched Jack furiously reeling in the slack. The shark went on several more runs, and Jack followed it around the boat.

"I guess this shark's the next big challenge for me," he said, keeping his line clear of obstructions. "Then I'll have to go skydiving or lion hunting or something. Maybe I'll join the French Foreign Legion."

Andrew tried to stand again. He found he could move his legs now, but only an inch or two. He watched Jack battling the shark, constantly letting line out and reeling it in. After nearly an hour, Jack seemed to be tiring. Andrew could feel some of his own strength returning.

"You . . . are . . . mine," Jack gasped as he leaned the rod back, bending it nearly double. He leaned forward, reeled the slack, then leaned back once again. His face had gone beet red, and sweat was pouring down it. "It's you or me, shark," he said, nearly out of breath. "Who you rooting for, Andy boy? Me or the shark?"

He leaned his rod back again and the mako lept from the water this time. Andrew heard it crash down. He noted the sharpening angle of Jack's line, an indication of the narrowing gap between the shark and the boat.

"Makos are one of the only sharks that can jump out of

the water," Jack said. "But I'm sure you already knew that, Fisher Boy."

He then clicked on the drag brake to prevent the shark from taking any more line, an arrogant gesture.

"No more runs for you, big guy!" he called to it, ready for a showdown. He turned to Andrew. "If you've never seen a man take a monster mako alone, you're about to see it now."

The shark made another dash. With the drag locked, it was able to yank Jack forward, slamming him up against the gunwale. Jack managed to hold onto the rod, which looked ready to snap. He tried to release the brake, but the line was too tight. The shark kept pulling, bending Jack and his rod over the gunwale.

"You . . . are . . . not . . . going . . . to . . . win," he said, trying to right himself.

But he couldn't. The power and weight of the mako were proving too much for him.

"Let go," Andrew said, not loud enough for Jack to hear. "Let go the rod."

Jack grabbed it higher up instead, and for a moment it looked like he might be able to pull it back. But the shark ran again and Andrew watched Jack, still holding the rod, being pulled over the gunwale. He heard the splash as he hit the water, then Jack yelling through a mouthful of it.

"You're not going to beat me, shark! I'm Jack Hawker! No one beats Jack Hawker!"

Andrew rolled onto his stomach and pushed himself to his knees. He crawled over to the side, grabbed onto the gunwale and mustered enough strength to pull himself up and look over it. He saw Jack in the water, still clutching the pole, the shark towing him behind it. "I'm coming to get you, shark!" Jack yelled after it. "It's you against me! And you're going to lose! Because I'm Jack fucking Hawker! Don't you even know who I am?"

The shark stopped, as though it had heard Jack and understood his taunts. It swam a wide circle until its dorsal was aimed directly its tormentor. It paused for a moment, then started toward him, in no particular rush. Jack let go of the rod and, to Andrew's shock and amazement, he began to swim toward the shark, his furious strokes punching the air and the water, as though preparing to fight it with his fists. The shark sped up, steadily closing the gap between them, its dorsal cleaving the water.

"Come on, shark!" Jack yelled, thrashing toward it. "Come on!"

Andrew watched until only a few yards separated them. Then he released his grip on the gunwale and let himself fall back to the deck. He covered his ears.

CHAPTER 31

Andrew stood in the parking lot outside Moran's, looking through the window. He watched Katie pulling the plugs on the neon beer signs inside. He saw the Michelob sign go dark, followed by the Budweiser sign, then the Heineken. He knew she was alone. None of her customers ever stayed until closing. He kept watching as she cleaned the last of the dirty glasses, then put the empty beer bottles in their respective cases, then began to wipe the bar with a clean rag. He felt nervous, standing out there, trying to think of what to say to her when he went in. He touched the bandage on the back of his head. The wound beneath it still felt raw and his head still ached. He went to the door and hesitated before pushing it open.

The bar looked especially dim with only the lights behind the top shelf bottles still on. Katie stopped wiping the bar.

"Andrew, what are you doing here?"

"I came to see you."

"Oh . . . Well, hi. How's it going?"

"It's going okay."

"Want a Heineken while I clean up?"

"How about a Bud?"

Katie opened a bottle of Budweiser and put it on the bar across from Andrew's stool. Andrew sat and tried to pay, but Katie wouldn't let him. She continued wiping and Andrew looked up at the swordfish over the bar.

"Do you remember when I caught that swordfish, Katie?"

Katie stopped wiping and looked up at it.

"August 19th, 1985."

"You have a good memory."

"It's hard to forget that one."

"I think I caught it with a surface popper."

"It was a bucktail. You caught it fifteen miles off the Point. It took two hours to bring in and you drank eight beers afterward."

"I could have sold it for a lot of money."

"I'm glad you didn't. I needed something to cover these ugly walls."

Andrew restrained the urge to reach over the bar and take her hand in his.

"How's business been, Katie?"

"Same as always. Slow, but steady."

"That's good."

Katie shrugged.

"Could be worse. How's the movie? You going to do another after this?"

"I'm through with movies and all that," Andrew said. "I came to tell you."

"Why?"

"Lots of reasons."

"I meant, why did you come tell me?"

A lump formed in Andrew's throat. He waited until it dissolved.

"Because I wanted you to know."

Katie seemed slightly perplexed, not quite sure how to interpret this.

"Listen, I'm sorry about the other night," she said.

"I'm the one who should be sorry."

"Why don't we just call it even?"

Andrew drank some beer and looked around the bar. It seemed different, but he couldn't figure out exactly what had changed. He looked at Katie again and noticed she was frowning at him.

"Andrew, what happened to your head?"

"Oh, nothing. I was fishing today. Tripped over some net."

"You've never done anything like that before."

"I guess I'm rusty."

"It's not serious, is it?"

"The doctor says I'll be fine."

"That's good. So, you're a fisherman again."

"Until the day I die."

"If you keep tripping over nets, that might be sooner than you think."

Katie came from behind the bar and sat on the stool next to Andrew.

"Turn around," she said. "Let me take a look at it."

Andrew turned so Katie could see the bandage better. Slowly, Katie peeled the adhesive away from his skin and leaned close enough for him to feel her breath against the back of his neck.

"Still hurt, Andrew?"

"A little. How's it look?"

"I've seen prettier sights."

Katie smoothed the bandage back in place and, to Andrew's surprise, she kissed it.

"Does that make it feel better?" she said.

Andrew's throat began to close again, and he suddenly felt like weeping.

"A lot better," he said, maintaining his composure.

"Are you hungry?"

"Starving."

"I'll ring out the register and we can go back to my house. I owe you a dinner. You still like steak, don't you?"

"I love steak."

She smoothed the bandage some more, then went around to the register and began counting the money in it. Andrew watched her the whole time, the pain in his head beginning to ease. When Katie finished counting, she turned around and their eyes met. This time neither of them looked away.

EPILOGUE

In October, a class four hurricane roared up the East Coast and slammed into Long Island. The storm had begun as a low pressure system rising from the hot plains of central Africa. It moved west from there and across the Atlantic, gathering energy from the water warmed by the long summer. Somewhere between the continents, it began to spin and rile the ocean below, creating waves that would travel thousands of miles before smashing into land.

No two hurricanes follow the same exact path. This one dipped south and hit the Caribbean islands first, flattening huts and killing ten in Haiti and the Dominican Republic before moving on to Puerto Rico, where four people died. It passed through Cuba next, its winds increasing from ninety miles an hour to a hundred. There it stalled for several hours, drenching the island and adding three to its toll. As it moved up to Florida, people as far north as Maine began to watch the Weather Channel, keeping it on while they ate dinner and did household chores.

The hurricane hugged the seaboard as it moved north. Most of the people in its path evacuated inland, gathering in schools and municipal buildings. The few foolish souls who stayed put watched their homes being destroyed, their cars being swamped, and their boats being carried off to sea or bashed to kindling against the docks.

The hurricane vented its fury on everyone and everything it encountered. It didn't quit after grinding through Florida. It wrought havoc in Georgia and the Carolinas, then Virginia, the Delmarva Peninsula and New Jersey. It appeared to be headed straight for New York City, but bounced off the belly-like curve of the Jersey coast and headed toward the eastern end of Long Island.

The year-round residents of the Hamptons and Montauk and the North Fork towns awaited its arrival, bracing for landfall. The summer people had long ago returned to the safety of New York City. Still, they tracked the storm on TV, hoping it might spare their summer houses. More than a few checked their home insurance policies to make sure premiums had been paid.

The hurricane stayed its course, landing in the middle of the night, whipping waves to fifteen feet and more. They pounded the ocean beaches, rushing over the dunes, breaking them down and carrying them away. The winds toppled trees and telephone poles, ripped roofs off houses and wrenched houses from their foundations. The surge flooded streets, turning them into canals. As the storm passed over the island on its way to New England, its eye gave brief respite before the winds hit again with even greater force. A man in the Springs died of a heart attack. A woman in West Hampton drowned when the ocean pulled her beach house off its stilts. But most had evacuated or moved to higher ground. It could have been worse.

The storm left after five hours. An eerie calm followed, and in the morning, the sun shone down from a brilliant blue sky. Many went down to the beach, driven there by some primal instinct rather than any logic or reason. They found much of the sand washed away. What remained had been packed to the consistency of concrete by the waves.

The East End had been hit hard, but most of the fishing boats were not completely destroyed. The fishermen repaired them quickly and resumed fishing as soon as possible. And to their surprise, they found that striped bass were running again, in great numbers. They brought them in by the thousands, on lines and in nets. They filled their holds and the dock freezers to overflowing. No one knew why the stripers had reappeared. Some said it had to do with the hurricane-altered currents. Most didn't try to explain it, though, fearful that doing so might jinx the run. And as the East End slowly repaired itself, it seemed that the fishermen there had found their place again. To them, it was as if the storm had restored some natural order to the island, some balance, at least for the time being.